I WANT TO BE A WRITER

I0622214

HIMESH DASH

First published in 2018 by

Becomeshakespeare.com

Wordit Content Design & Editing Services Pvt. Ltd.
Unit - 26, Building A -1,
Nr Wadala RTO, Wadala (East), Mumbai 400037,
India T: +91 8080226699

Wordit Art Fund helps deserving authors publish their
work by providing monetary support.
To apply for funding, please visit us at
www.BecomeShakespeare.com

DEDICATED TO

⚛ ⚛ ⚛

To my teachers, friends and parents

PROLOGUE

He was ready with a cup of cold coffee with ice cubes floating around. He skittered over a small wooden armless chair and sat on it comfortably. The room was contained with sunlight glooming inside through the wet windows. He took a sip, and after a short interval of preparations, the interview started.

A sweet young girl with curved eyebrows and a piece make-up with a mic and a camera on her side glanced. "So, Mr Kabir Malhotra, the youngest bestseller of India at the age of 16. And now your fourth book *I Know My Limits* is getting excellent reviews all over the country. So, how are you?"

"Still alive, I guess."

"Okay! So how it feels to see such huge readers loving your novels?"

Kabir cleared his throat and said, "It really feels good."

She hissed, "Okay. We all know about your novels, it's quite connecting and healthy. So, what's new about this novel?"

Kabir patted his thighs and confessed, "It's about a boy who believes that he has no limits, no weakness, no impotence and, above all, he has no powers. He tries to prove his potential but loses his near ones and tries to find out the hidden secrets of his existence."

She smiled. "Great!"

The interviewer scratched her eyebrow with her index finger and looked at him. "So, you started writing at the age of 16 and gave us a brilliant tale. But how you got such an inspiration? And all about it. How you got that desire for writing a novel?"

Kabir's eyes went down for a second, and he asked frankly, "Have you read my first novel?"

She chuckled. "Ya, of course."

Kabir came close to her and whispered, "Then, you must ask Arun about it. He knows more than me." Arun was Kabir's fictional character in his debut novel.

She appreciated. "Great answer." They exchanged glances, and Kabir was happy with that.

He advised, "But, mam, it really needs a strong, sorry, a quite strong determination and consistency to achieve a writing."

She nodded. "Ya"

She added looking at him, "So, your first book was a fictional one."

Kabir nodded. "But is inspired by true events."

"Well, I want to know what's your actual story if you don't mind, and about Tara too. Your best friend to whom you dedicated all your novels." Her voice was becoming low in a descending order towards the last.

He wetted his lips. "Mam, you better don't ask those questions."

She pleased him, and Kabir had no other choice to accept it.

He closed his eyes and a number of scenes flashed across his eyes. He winked as the sunlight was falling right on his face. He hissed, and his mind recaptured all his memories. Thinking of his past made him happily sad. The glittering eyes came out of soft tears which was sparkling on sunlight dews. He looked at the ceiling to hold his tears and smiled. He gasped…

CHAPTER 1

The day was great, the class was great, the weather was great, everything was fine except those annoying teachers. It was almost a soothing sunny day! The bright sun tore the vast bluish sky and made all the faces to relax (except one). Squeaking, the calcium carbonate crushed over the blackboard. The wrecked bins filled of crushed papers and paper airplanes though seemed more than a tidy classroom.

And then a teen sat on the corner of the room. On the wooden carved bench, his eyes looked at the bright sky to relax his body. He had a great time, stretched his hands to his cheeks and lay down over his maths book, and he slept as usual. The yellow light quietly flashed over his face, and he was comfortable dreaming to his own senses. Everything around him was so calm, so silent, so yellowish.

But it was a kind of silence before any disaster.

"Roll No 11, stand up. And tell me the answer." Suddenly his Roll No encountered his sleep.

"Huh?" But nothing went to his ears. No reply, no answer, just a sudden sense of distortion.

"Roll No 11!" she screamed.

"Yes sir. I…I…I mean, madam." With a great abstraction, he stood up and responded with a disturbed mind and a disrupted sleep.

Students around him started laughing, whereas he was still in a state of distraction, scratching his head with suspicion. The jocular sounds were hearing very strange and supernatural to him. His vision blurred, so he flicked his head, cleared his eyes and soon he revived that the teacher with her 18-inch steel scale is coming; leaping it over her palm.

She pointed and quizzed him, "So, Mr Kabir Malhotra. Can you please explain me, what's going on?" she clinched his ear and made him stand outside before Kabir could explain her anything.

Fortune favoured him, as the bell rang, and it proved to be a good companion of Kabir. It always handed him from his menace. "Oh, God!" Kabir exhaled with an air of relaxation.

The whole world that was in a slow path of boredom made a great pace with every footstep of students dribbling.

But Kabir was busy with his cogitative mood. What was he thinking with his fixed eyes staring at the sky? Well, nobody knows. After a silence, from his back, he heard, "Where were you man?"

It's Krish, another friend of Kabir with good and safe hands. He met him when he was in fifth standard. Krish is a smart, although a foolish, guy whose utmost dream is to surf his bike at 100 miles in first gear. He is kind yet would leave anyone for cricket. Cricket is his heart, and his heart is in cricket.

"Okay, leave it. It's going to be late after all. Are you not coming?" said Bob.

Bob is his another fellow. His description needs a lengthy cloth similar to his belly. His hunger can't be controlled by anyone on this earth except by him. His desire is to be slim and trim and to have lots and lots of girlfriends (impossible).

All the three are kinda good friends.

"Huh?" Kabir was busy with his books.

"Let's go, Kabir. It's been late," Krish said.

Bob, blossomed by his thought, said, "Yesterday I saw a girl. WOW! So cute, so sweet, I must say."

"Kabir, let's go now." Krish couldn't control his strength.

Kabir lifted his bag and said, "Okay fine, let's go. But, wait, you have to answer a question of mine."

Kabir hit Bob to come to the present and he nodded.

Both accepted the dare. And Kabir looked at them and questioned, *"I am like impossible, but still*

I am possible. I can do anything, if I am determined. Nothing can stop me, neither storms nor luck. Who am I?"

Bob said, "Once more."

Kabir nodded.

Their minds were spaghettified by Kabir's black hole question.

"Think! But don't bite off more than you can chew." Kabir made his books, chained his bag and left, leaving a qualm for Krish and Bob.

Krish scratched his head and looked foolish. He consulted Bob, but he was in his own cute world. He failed to notice when Kabir left the place. "Hey, Kabir, wait for me." Krish handed Bob's hand and sprinted on his way to catch Kabir on the road. He gasped. "Hey, Kabir, I surrender. What's the answer?"

"Leave it."

In the middle of the yellowish road, Krish again called off. "Tell me na, Kabir, please."

"Okay, answer me. In this whole universe, is there anything impossible?"

"No, the word itself says I am possible. I have read it many times." Krish showed his competence over his confidence.

"How can we achieve this greatness?" Kabir stretched his eyebrows.

"Simple, if one is self-determined," Bob answered now.

"Good. So, is there anything that can hurdle you once you are strongly determined?"

"No, nothing can."

"Who am I?" looking at Krish, Kabir queered.

"You are…" Krish made a pause and reminded. He was shocked by his simplicity and smiled at himself with a little sigh.

Kabir walked again, which was again unnoticed by Krish.

"Hey, Kabir, wait na."

Kabir was irritated by the same orders of Krish, the fourth time. "How you got such a ridiculous idea?"

Kabir put his hands over Krish's right shoulder and gaped. "Listen, I…"

He was cut by many crackling sound, and they looked and saw Bob with a pack of chips.

"Leave that bear, Kabir. Say."

"Ya, I observe many people every day. What I found common between all is that they are still the victims of their past. My neighbour Bhattacharya aunty always remains sad because she lost her cat Romeo in a road accident. I don't know if that cat can be recovered or not, but for a lost hope we should not be sad.

"We should learn to live in the present. Just look at the riddle, the question was too simple, and the rest was to make us confused. That's all."

"Your thoughts are simply clever, Kabir."

"But don't you forget, day after tomorrow we must submit our assignment, which is hard enough, long enough, impossible enough to complete it by tomorrow."

"Is it a reminder or a warning!"

Krish smiled and said, "Perhaps, a warning."

Without answering his query, Kabir walked firmly and smiled. "But, don't you worry."

His relaxing words are really scaring after all. Krish thought and questioned him, "Why?"

Bob took a pause from his chips and said, "I know, he is gonna die today due to lots and lots of riddles."

Bob and Krish laughed. But it didn't interest Kabir.

Kabir walked and jumped slightly forward and backed with joy and said, "You, dumbo! Day after tomorrow is my birthday."

*

Kabir reached home with an aspiration, a doubt and a sweat-filled body. An aspiration of being released by the hands of Miss Pussy and a doubt whether he is going to die today or not.

He jumped into the sofa. He turned on the TV and glanced over his favourite show, *K for Knowledge*. It is a show headed by some documentaries and films. Suddenly, the screen went black, and Kabir raised his eyebrow. He turned over and saw his elegant mother with a shrunken face.

"Mom, what's your problem?"

"First go and get ready for lunch. Fast."

"Mom..." He was cut midway. "Just go." Kabir had no other choice but to take a long bath.

His mom, Priya Malhotra, is nevertheless a great housewife and a mother. She is good at maths and quite sensitive when it comes to relationships.

It was five in the evening, and Kabir saw Bob and Krish with their bicycles, staring at him.

"Kabir, let's go, everyone is there." From the window, he couldn't utter a word but signalled them to wait.

Kabir looked towards his mom who was reading the newspaper. "Mom, Krish is in danger. It's urgent. Don't ask."

"Hey, Kab—" And he ran.

"Krish, you can do it!" All were cheering up from the side. Kabir was on the other end praying for a win. It was a 10-over match. The other team had made 99. So, as 100 was their target, Krish was under pressure.

However, Kabir got bowled after playing a good innings. After eight overs, they were 74 for 5. Krish was still there on the crease with Bob, making runs throughout the turf. "Krish, be at your position and take a single in the last ball." Kabir shouted from the so-called stands.

In the end, they needed seven runs in two balls. Bob was on strike. "Bob, just see the ball and hit it. I will run, okay?"

"Okay."

Bob managed to touch the ball, while Krish had to dive on the ground to take a single. It was a heart-burning situation. The sweat and eagerness were there on all their faces. Krish took a long breath and tapped his bat (a do-or-die situation).

The bowler raced towards Krish and bowled the ball with high intensity. No one knew what would happen. The ball boomed three times. And it was over.

The ball hit the ground and then Krish pulled his bat up and dragged it from his back and punched the ball out of the stands.

"And Dhoni finishes off in style!" Kabir stood up.

"Well done, buddy!" They all cheered for Krish, and no doubt, it was one of his best innings.

After so-called meeting ceremony, Kabir reached home and found his father curling his hand over his ankle, sitting. "Where were you?" Kabir's dad is really a sweet father, who works hard and earns for his family. No doubt, they weren't neither rich nor poor but quite good.

"C'mon, Dad, we won the match."

"So, what was your contribution?"

"Huh? Actually, I gave my best support to the team. Although I got out making 14 runs, I did really cheer for my team."

"Good then, go and do your homework." Kabir's father was always straightforward with a less product of sensitivity and a heart.

The night went out with a great sweet sleep. And Kabir dreamt of a new thought.

CHAPTER 2

"Mom, I am home."

Nothing was for sure, interesting in the class that day, or he didn't want to.

"MOM!"

Kabir couldn't hear anything. So, he emptied his legs and went inside, grabbing the strips of his bag.

"Mom, are you not there?"

He suspected and shouted twice. Still the silence paced his home. So, he walked slowly to the dining room and found something unusual. Nobody was there. It puzzled him, as it was that time of the day where her mom usually sipped tea every day.

He went upstairs. When he neared his room, he saw his door unlocked. It was the second event of the day that puzzled him. (He always locks his room before he goes to school and hides the key in a secretive place that only he and his partner knows.) So, he with a little faith went closer to his room and pushed the door with a quick jab, only to find himself welcomed by a great surprised voice.

"Welcome home, partner."

The voice and the fruitful words made Kabir to identify the person. He was none other than his 46-year-old partner from the USA, Uncle Iyer. He was a kind and fun-loving man. His black-rimmed spectacles over his white face with small white noodles-like beard suited him well.

"Ahh, partner. I was waiting for your return," Kabir silently sneered.

Uncle Iyer never likes when anybody calls him by his name, Iyer. That's why he and Kabir decided to call themselves as partners. But moreover, they were like partners.

They both held each other's hands, whacked it, tickled it and smacked it, a kind of pleasure gesture. Then they hugged gently.

"And, partner, please hold your socks back and get it washed. It was really a mess to get your keys out of that secret place," Uncle Iyer snorted.

Kabir guffawed with tears of emotions stuck in his eyes like a dam holding the water.

"I really missed you, partner." Kabir hugged him once again, showing his true feelings.

"Okay, okay. But listen, I am here only for you. Tomorrow you are having your birthday. So, for that I have a surprise for you!"

Kabir claimed excitedly, "I knew it. Yes, I knew it. You know what, partner? From yesterday I was only dreaming about you, that Uncle Iyer will come and surprise me with a surprise. And it worked. You see.

"So, where is that kind of present?"

"Not now, pal. At 12o'clock, sharp."

"Over now? Kabir, go and get freshen up soon. And come for lunch. Clear now." Breaking the discourse, her mother ordered him precisely and went out of the room collecting his dirty laundry.

"It's in their gene to send their children to bath." Iyer laughed and nodded.

Kabir took a towel and put it on his shoulder. At the bathroom's entrance, he added, "Okay, partner, till I get freshen up, have a cup of coffee. Then, I will share more of my interesting stories."

Iyer interrupted and joked, narrowing his eyes, "Your story! Why—I mean, how?" Uncle Iyer finished his sentence with a funny question.

Kabir said shyly, "Stop pulling my leg!" With a smile, Kabir locked the door hardly and went to get refreshed. Uncle Iyer's eyes wandered around the room, and after a while he went downstairs to have his coffee.

Kabir bathed and came down to have lunch.

"Let's start," he said, taking his seat. After lunch both the partners jumped on the sofa and talked about various topics—teachers' funny names, the USA, cricket, their last meeting, their change in tastes and habits, movies, dreams, cars. Probably about everything.

Uncle Iyer got exhausted as time walked away. He took out his black-rimmed spectacles, slid his head upon the sofa and took a sweet nap.

Once lunch was over, afternoon flew by too. But Kabir waited for the arrival of midnight.

He was just expecting a great kind of stuff that will give him a sense of bliss and satisfaction. And finally, the time came, the clock struck 12. And Kabir hurried to his partner's room and knocked the door. "Partner, hurry up, it's 12. Partner…"

Uncle Iyer opened the door, and seeing him, Kabir excitedly asked, "My gift, partner."

"Oh!" Uncle Iyer remembered the occasion and presented him a cuboidal shaped wrapper. "Happy birthday, partner, and here, it is your present."

Kabir snatched the gift and tore the wrapping as if a treasure was buried deep under it. But who knew that this present would become a great achievement tool for him in the future. He was curious as he handled the gift with his gentle hands.

Kabir was transfixed for a few seconds, gaping at the present.

And with a deep breath, Kabir asked, "Seriously? A book!" Kabir was disappointed, as he never expected such a piece of gift. He returned the book and dashed to his room.

"Hey, partner. Wait. Listen." Uncle Iyer took the book and hurried before him to his room. Kabir was truly sad.

Uncle Iyer had a look at his room and saw Kabir on his bed much to his chagrin. "Hey, partner. Are you not going to have it?"

There was no answer, silence pervaded the room.

But Uncle Iyer stepped forward towards Kabir and sat closer to him. He then put his soft and gentle hand over Kabir's shoulder and said, "Hey…p…partner. I know it's not that kind of present what you have expected. But, believe me, it's more than that of your expectation."

Kabir finally broke his silence, and Uncle Iyer felt relieved. "Sorry, partner. But seriously…I…I just hate such stuffs, especially those novels," said Kabir.

"But why, partner? Okay, you just give me one good reason to not read it and I will give you one thousand better reasons why you must."

"I…I…don't know, partner. I just feel it's boring. When I was small, I always tried my best to have it, but I failed, and from that time, reading is just a past devil for me."

Uncle Iyer felt relaxed and made it with his speech, saying "You are now small too. So, for my sake, just try it once more. You know what?When I was small, I also used to hate books, and of course, those strange books without pictures, the novels, really tortured me a lot. But when I tried to read once, during the first time, my perseverance ended up with failure, so I tried once more. And I still failed. But what I earned from it was patience. First of all, we need patience to have anything we want. And, my partner, you have already earned it. So, why not one more time. Listen, it's a kind of gift, more than a friend. Have it, try it, and share it, if you like it."

Uncle Iyer didn't get any reply. Kabir was slightly mesmerised by his words, though he intended to listen to his mind.

"Hmm…then. I am leaving this book here. If you want, you can take the book. Good night, partner." Uncle Iyer left the door ajar and fled the scene.

Kabir breathed a sigh of relief as held the book. It was written *The Journey of a Child* by Meera Sharma. He flipped through the pages, and by its texture and smell, he grew quite fond of the book. Suddenly, his inner conscience made him to try the book. (Maybe he really wanted to.) And soon he started reading the novel.

The night went through, and Uncle Iyer was still sleeping, occupied with his dreams. All of a sudden, he heard a knocking sound, increasingly clearer and louder with every passing second. He got irritated. As he woke, he looked at the clock, and it was 6:30 am. He wore his spectacles and opened the door, yawning.

It was Kabir.

"Huh?"

Before Uncle Iyer could say anything, Kabir squeaked, "Thanks, partner, for such a great gift. It's…it's really amazing. And the writer Meera Sharma. Woo! She was just superb. Her way of writing, and the story was brilliant. I must—I'm in love with her writing. Thanks, pal."

"Are you serious?" Uncle Iyer raised his brow doubtfully.

"About what, partner?" said Kabir.

"Ar…Are you serious? You completed the whole book in one night!" His eyes darted on Kabir. (It was approximately a 250-page book.)

Kabir raised his shoulders proudly and said, "Yup. I did."

Uncle Iyer was fascinated, his eyes dazzling. He blinked his eyes to clear the wetness of happy tears and told him in a satisfied tone, "Good to see you that you liked it."

The smile on both of their faces was unstoppable. After a short interval, breaking his smile, Kabir pronounced, "Okay, partner, I need to go."

"Where?"

"Of course, school. I am having my birthday today," said Kabir with heart full of happiness.

Riding on his bicycle, he waved to his partner. "See you then, partner."

CHAPTER 3

Kabir got well dressed and readied for his arrival at school as it was showtime. As like the previous day, the weather was fine with clear blue sky that day.

In the school, two of his fellow mates wished him, "Happy birthday, Kabir."

"Thanks bros."

"You're welcome, but seriously with this outfit of blue denim jeans, a black blazer upon a white shirt, you are looking awesome. I dare you many of the girls are gonna die for you," Krish teased him.

"Ha. Thanks, but no thanks, I don't want to put so many lives in danger," Kabir cross-answered.

"Girls! Where are they? Hey, Kabir?" Bob enquired.

"Ha-ha.... Well, may be." Krish and Kabir posted a smile. "But what I see? Haven't you slept last night?" Krish questioned by narrowing his eyes.

"Oh. That's a long *Journey of a Child*."

"Huh?"

"Oh, I forgot to tell you. Last night, I got a book as a gift from my partner. You well know him. And I read the book the whole night. And believe me, it is the best book I have ever read. Of course, the author, Meera Sharma, is fantastic. She is so good with her writing, especially dialogue writing," Kabir replied with great pleasure.

"Meera Sharma! I have heard about her a lot. She is one of the bestselling author in India. And she has also won many—"

"Is she hot?" Bob asked.

They all laughed.

"So, Bob, what about your assignment?"

He smelled the air and said, "Huh? Ya, I forgot to bring it." Krish was okay with his assignment, and Kabir was behind schedule, incomplete with his assignment.

The teacher entered the class without warning with her trademark 18-inch steel scale leaping out of her palm. Kabir and Krish occupied their seats, and the class wished the teacher a very good morning.

"I don't think your morning is going to be good enough. Show me your assignments. Hurry up!" Miss Pussy did what she was always best at with her badass behaviour. Everybody hurriedly opened their bags and searched for their assignments like someone hoping to find petrol in the place of digging.

Miss Pussy sat on her seat with contempt. She said sarcastically, "Hurry up! Roll No1, come with your assignment."

Akash was the first in line. And he submitted his assignment with no qualms, being as proud as a peacock. And up to Roll No9, it got over without any confusion.

Kabir was ready with his ICBM excuse.

"Roll No10," the teacher called.

Giya's face looked dull. She gritted her teeth and clenched her jaw, and her legs started to shiver.

"Giya, where is your assignment?"

The spine-chilling voice made her body tremble with fear as she still had no answer.

"I asked you, 'Where is your assignment?'."

"Ma…Mam…I…I forgot to bring it."

"So, should I go and bring it? What were you doing at home? Can't you follow your timetable? Should I complain it to the principal? Wait, let me talk to your parents. They will better care about you and with your performance."

"So…Sorry, madam." Her mouth was twitching.

"I hate the word *sorry*. Stretch your hand."

Giya cried out, "I'm really sorry, madam."

Miss Pussy, with her 18-inch steel scale, hit her soft palm with great brutality showing her repressed anger.

Giya shuddered with a huge cry as her fear was now reduced to tears, breaking her heart.

"No one is going to be excused today. Got it?"

Seeing this from a distance, Kabir thought, *God, help me! She is gonna kill me.*

"Roll No11. Oh, sorry. Kabir Malhotra." (She shouted, remembering her words from the previous day.)

Kabir stood up, inching his jeans downwards. "Mam, act...actually...I...I—"

The peon entered the classroom and gave a notice. "Kabir Malhotra."

"Yes."

"Principal Sir is calling you."

He went with the peon and was back after 15 minutes.

"May I come in, mam?"

"C'mon. What's the matter?" Miss Pussy narrowed her eyes, gaping at Kabir.

"OH, he wanted to congratulate me. Actually, I bagged the first prize in a state-level painting competition, and got selected for the national painting competition, competing with other 29 states."

The teacher was glad to hear such a great news.

"Kabir, come here."

"Mam, I forgot to complete my assignment." Kabir heartbeat increased rapidly with every footstep he inched towards her.

Miss Pussy greeted him with a handshake and said, "It's okay. You can submit later. Students, see. Kabir showed his talent. He proved himself and made our school proud. All should learn from him. Now, congratulate Kabir."

For a second, Kabir looked like a fool beside her, and his heartbeat returned to normal as he thanked God for his miracle.

"Good charm, Kabir," Krish and Bob whispered.

Kabir returned home safely, and he was quite happy with a sad news that Bob was made to kneel down before the class.

"I am home, Mom."

"Keep your socks in the right place, Kabir."

Uncle Iyer asked him about his day, handing a chilled glass of water.

"Thanks, pal."

"Believe me, it was great. And there's good news too!" Kabir told him about his achievement, and about Bob's punishment too.

"Woo. What a great gift on your birthday!" Uncle Iyer giggled. They talked about the match, Iyer narrating his story of birthdays and blah, blah, blah.

"Kabir, go and get ready soon. And come to collect your stuff." Kabir looked at Iyer and gasped, "It's all in their genes."

Lunch was over and evening came along. And it was time for his birthday celebration. The party was arranged in the house and was decorated with balloons and streamers.

Everybody came: his friends, his teachers, and all his classmates and relatives. He blew out the candles and cut the cake, while Krish burst the balloon and Bob blew the party blowers. He turned 16. Everybody greeted him with gifts. He got an artist set of acrylic and oil painting colours from Krish, which was pre-planned.

"Thanks, Krish."

"My pleasure."

"So, Kabir, what you want on your birthday?" his dad asked him, making everyone else in the crowd silent.

Kabir looked everybody, but his eyes wandered towards his partner, Uncle Iyer.

He opened his heart and said, "Mom and Dad, I want books."

Everybody in the guest was startled.

"Yes, Son. Why not?" said his dad with a great smile and hugged him. Everybody enjoyed the party.

There was a graffiti wall arrangement made, where Kabir found strange but two interesting notes—drawings and signs. Someone had written about improving his studies, which Kabir guessed was Miss Pussy. And there was a sign "Enjoy Partner!" with a smiley written at the side.

CHAPTER 4

It was Sunday morning; when the world was sleeping at peace, a terrific war was happening inside the house.

"C'mon, Roger. You can do it. Ahh! Reload, reload. Hurry up. Now, fireeee!" Kabir was shouting in high-pitched voice upon controlling his joystick.

"Ha. You can't break through my shield," Uncle Iyer murmured.

"Yup. Ya…good…good… No…no…no. No. Not that way."

"Game Over," a metallic voice pronounced from the computer screen. "Shit! Partner, if I would have given one more chance, then definitely I'd have hit you." Kabir challenged his partner.

"Okay, whatever you say. Let's start." Uncle Iyer accepted the challenge, and both held their joystick to fight for their respect. They were playing the number one ranked PC game, BORN TO FIGHT.

Kabir rubbed his nose to show his proud of honour over his partner. Although both were partners, sometimes they had to play apart to enjoy togetherness.

Both skilfully manoeuvred their joysticks through their deft fingers and hooted with their exciting voice. "Ya…Good. Not again. Yup… Rogerrrrr! Shoot!" Kabir became furious and answered his partner bitterly with a headshot.

"Here I go." Uncle Iyer was little bit nervous and doubted his strength. *Come on, Iyer, you can beat him; after all, you are a 46-year-old experienced old man,* he thought.

The two were struggling hard to overtake one another.

Suddenly, Uncle Iyer thought of last night. While moving his fingers over the joystick, Uncle Iyer appreciated, "By the way, partner, last night you were really impressive, I must say. The way you demanded for books was brilliant."

"Thanks, but, partner, I want only Meera Sharma's. Come on, Roger!" he replied, tapping over his joystick.

Both the gamers all of a sudden heard a knocking sound not in the virtual world but in real world. Kabir paused the game and said, "I'll just come, partner."

He hurried through the dining room and opened the door. "Yes."

"Saurav Malhotra?" the man asked. "Yup, I'm his son. But he isn't present right now," said Kabir.

"We have a courier for his name," the man said, pointing towards a large parcel. It was cuboidal-shaped cardboard-covered box.

Seeing that parcel Kabir thought, *I don't think Dad have so much work to do with such large stuffs. But still he works.*

"Okay, Uncle, hand it over to me," Kabir said politely.

"Yup. Sir, your signature. Here," the man said, presenting the service paper in a gentle manner.

Kabir searched for the pen but was readily given one from the courier man. "Here it goes. And over." Wetting his lips, Kabir returned the paper. "Thanks, sir."

"You're welcome, and one more thing, very important one. Ah...hmm..." Kabir said, tapping his finger over his forehead remembering something.

"Yes sir. Any problem?"

"Ya. Don't call me 'Sir'. You can call me...just Kabir." Kabir said with a smile, showing all his teeth.

The man smiled and said, "Sure, sir—sorry, I mean, Kabir."

"Have a nice day."

The man left the place, keeping the parcel at the door front.

"It's so massive and heavy too," Kabir grumbled, dragging the fully loaded cardboard box to the dining room, and Uncle Iyer saw it—a large gift-wrapped cuboidal-shaped box.

Kabir unwrapped the parcel slowly and steadily through the sides. Uncle Iyer gave one of his secretive smiley look. *Kabir don't know what kind of treasure is inside,* Uncle Iyer thought.

As Kabir uncovered one of the cardboard folding, he found a photo with a title on the cover.

Looking downwards, he read the name: it was Meera Sharma.

For a moment, he was shocked and looked blank, but it was a different kind of blankness from the one he made when he received his first gift. He was totally amused to see the gift. It was a complete set of Meera Sharma's novels. "Is it true or I'm making fool of myself."

Uncle Iyer pinched him from his back to bring him back to normalcy.

Clearing his eyes, Kabir said, "Partner, it's true. It's true. I mean?" He was happy but doubtful, and high-five with his partner as he stopped for a moment to clear his mind.

"Wait, how my dad knew about Meera Sharma?" Uncle Iyer just smiled as usual. Seeing his smile, Kabir thought, *I got it.*

"Partner, it's you." It was Iyer who knew about Kabir's choice. Beaming with smile, Kabir chased Iyer to his room with a pillow in his hand. Uncle Iyer moved back to the dining room where they were gaming and stood on the sofa. Kabir was on his tender attacking spirit with his pillow. "Why didn't you tell me? Hey, here I go." Kabir threw the pillow.

"Okay, okay. Stop. Listen. I knew it that you really loved her writing and her story, that you are not going to read any other's. That's why I did that."

Kabir was quite glad to listen. He then hugged Uncle Iyer and thanked him.

On hugging him, Iyer whispered in his ears, "I don't know what is going to be with your Roger. But you're really going to lose."

"Ha! Let's see," answered Kabir, clearing his throat.

The two again resumed the game, holding their joysticks firmly.

CHAPTER 5

Kabir was riding a bicycle daily whose two tires were day and night. He finished reading half of the books within a week. He became very much fond of books. Seeing this, Iyer thought, *God. Thanks. Kabir is doing a great job.*

He was overwhelmed by Meera's novels. And soon she became his favourite. But who knew that for her he will change his destiny?

In Nagpur, as famous as oranges are, the weather is more or less similar. It was a Sunday, and the sky was bright and clear, but for Kabir, it was nothing more than a penny.

"Hey, Kabir. Let's go and play cricket. Looks like a great weather. Everybody has come. Hurry up," Krish called, with his cycle in tow.

"Sorry, Krish, I can't leave, it's the climax!" Kabir murmured from the couch, with a book in his hand.

"You and your Meera. Uff! Hmmm…But still, carry on. Okay then, see you later." Krish rode his cycle.

"Show me her photo," Bob gasped. Krish grabbed his hand and led him away.

Kabir returned to the sofa, his book-reading place that pulled him like a magnet. In one hand, he held the book and on the other, the remote. He switched on the television and tuned in to his favourite program, *K for Knowledge*. He was deeply engrossed in his book when he heard a sudden droning sound from the TV.

Here we have India's bestseller. Meera Sharma! the TV compere announced.

At first, he was irritated as the thunderous clapping sounds disturbed him, but when he heard that familiar name, he paused for a moment as everything was blank once again—his jaw lowered, his book fell down, and he was dumbstruck.

"Seriously...Meera Sharmaaaa! Woww!" Kabir thanked his fortune, and he was now glued to the television. For Kabir, this moment was worthier than her mom's whole jewellery set.

He cannot believe his own eyes and immediately called his partner.

"Yup, pal." Uncle Iyer ran down the stairs hurriedly looking for Kabir.

"Hurry up!" he shouted.

"Ya. What happened to you?" Iyer questioned him, seeing him standing so near to the LED TV monitor.

"Partner, partner, I want to meet Meera Sharma. I don't know how. I just want to meet her."

For a second, Iyer was confused. *Is he normal or anything untoward happened to him at school?* he thought.

"Partner, what are you thinking? I want to meet Meera Sharma," Kabir pleaded. At that moment, for Uncle Iyer, the demand made by Kabir looked like meeting an alien from the outer space. He wanted to laugh out loud but hesitated and stopped by seeing Kabir's innocence and simplicity.

Iyer tried to trick him and play a game. Of course, being a 46-year-old experienced man, he changed the topic through his great oratory skill.

Kabir had his eyes fixed on him, expecting a reply. Clearing his throat, Uncle Iyer said, "By the way, partner, why don't you go and play a match? The weather looks brilliant."

"Ya, Krish too asked me to join him." Uncle Iyer took a breath of comfort listening to his reply (without hearing his next sentence).

"But, partner, what about Meera Sharma?"

Drawing inspiration from everywhere, Iyer backed off and secretly motioned towards his room.

"Hey, partner, wait. Where are you going?" Kabir asked in an annoying tone.

Uncle Iyer took a second to think and got a brilliant idea to sum up the discussion. He drifted back silently and said, "Ha. Act...Actually, I was trying to...too...say you something."

"Ya, tell."

Uncle Iyer, licking his tongue and wetting his mouth, said, "Actually, I was thinking, instead of you meeting her, it'll be better if she comes and meets you."

"Is it possible, partner?" Kabir was astonished and surprised to hear Iyer's answer.

"Yup. Why not? But for that to happen, you must be capable and worthy of it." Kabir was perplexed by his statement.

"Stop beating around the bush, partner. Make it clear," said Kabir.

"I just want to say that, you do something different, something new I must say, so that the author would come to meet you, to congratulate you for your work."

Kabir eagerly listened to his speech, and his positivity helped him to stay level-headed. He asked Uncle Iyer for the help to achieve his mission.

"So, partner, for doing something new, as you said, what should I do?"

Uncle Iyer, even though irritated by his question, gave a life-changing suggestion.

"For that, Kabir, you have to write novels like her. So that one day you will become a bestseller. And, I bet you, that day when she will be there to meet you, you will have the greatest feeling of your lifetime. You will be proud of yourself. Everybody will be happy around you. And specially I will."

To see Kabir scrutinising his thought process, Uncle Iyer thought, *now he is fine. Good. Kabir was not ready to accept the idea.*

Uncle Iyer said, coughing, "That's why, Kabir. Leave it."

It was unbearable to see Kabir standing disappointed with lowered neck. So, Uncle Iyer said, "But, you can also e-mail her. I mean, if she has time, she may reply."

"Huh!" Kabir in a flash ran towards his laptop. He opened the mail app and started writing:

Dear Meera mam,

I'm Kabir, 16 years old. But mind you I'm your biggest fan. I have read every word and every line of your every book, almost ten times. My partner, whom I love the most, advised me to write a novel, so that you would come to meet me. But still, there's plan B which is to write you a mail.

So, Meera mam, I badly need to meet you, but I can't. I have many queries to ask, like why the child, Stephen, never gets old either in his long journey, whether he gets a home or not and blah, blah, blah. So, to solve my problems, can you please take out some time for me, if you don't mind, and come to my house? I'm eagerly waiting!

Kabir

"Good job, pal. Now, you just need to sit silently and wait."

The waiting game started as days and weeks went on. Being patiently waiting is one of the toughest job on earth, Kabir realised. And it was all over after waiting for two and half weeks; Kabir's patience finally burst out.

Kabir became a melted ice, as he lost his interest and patience within a short span of time, so he started watching *K for Knowledge*. Iyer, sitting beside him, was reading the news headlines.

Kabir Suddenly heard the TV compere announcing, *Meera Sharma is coming to Pune for her book launch tomorrow, in Histo Library at 5:30 pm.*

The withered face of Kabir soon blossomed with a great smile. He pointed out, "Partner, look. She is coming tomorrow. I want to meet her at any cost."

"As if you are earning?"

Uncle Iyer thought for a second, "Nagpur to Pune is 720 km. If we go by car, it will take hardly 13 hours. Let's see."

Kabir shook his hand and claimed, "Hey, partner, what are you calculating? I want to meet her."

Uncle Iyer, being himself a big fan of Meera, was ready for the travel and said, "Okay, then. But, first of all, I need to talk to your parents."

Kabir became too excited and cheerful. Kabir was quite fortunate as his parents agreed. He was on cloud nine. He soon got busy packing his bag with his books to get her signature. He also had many more plans besides taking selfies with her. His expectations were towering with sky being the limit.

"WHAT! I mean seriously. You are going to meet her."

Kabir nodded with a smile. "So lucky, man," Bob said.

"You can say that. By the way you two can come along," Kabir asked, breaking the chalks.

"I really wanted to, but I have my homework. Else, TOP." Krish nodded.

"Huh?"

"Terror of Pussy." They laughed, and Bob described his excuse of being busy with a new girl he found yesterday.

"Okay, Kabir. Happy journey!"

As evening came, Uncle Iyer parked the car near the footpath. His mother was teary-eyed, while his father, being straightforward, just warned him to be careful.

Kabir got the blessings from his parents and sat on the front seat of the car beside Uncle Iyer. Uncle Iyer ushered, "So, partner, let's go."

"Bye, Mom and Dad, love you."

And they fled. Kabir was just praying for a good ride as he knew that Uncle Iyer was a very bad driver. They listened to songs and had a good journey. As the darkness took over, Uncle Iyer stopped the car and looked for a restaurant. And he found one. They took the night's supper in The Cookplaza. They had good dinner with some snacks and gravy. Soon they were on the road. Kabir slept deeply after a long ride, and on the other hand, Uncle Iyer was trying his best to not sleep. He played FM radio and listened to comedy shows. It is impossible to feel sleepy when anyone is listening to comedies. So, somehow, they reached Pune at almost 8:00 am. Uncle Iyer drove at good speed, and he nudged Kabir slightly to awake him. Holding the steering wheel, Uncle Iyer said, "Hey, Kabir. Wake up. We are here."

Kabir with his tired eyes looked through the windshield. He felt the warmth of the sunlight that was right at his face. He yawned and looked at his partner and asked grumbled, "Partner, where are we?"

Uncle Iyer said with a smile, "We are in Pune, dude."

Nobody knew what happened to Kabir, but he looked like some kind of hyper ATP secretion flowed through his nerves, and he got in position with full power. Iyer was astonished to see his passion.

He took the corner like it was on rails. The car's vibration stopped, and Iyer went outside and looked around. This time he realised that "Nope."

He got inside the car with a sigh and took a deep breath to relax himself. He again started the engine and rode. Kabir, sitting beside him, asked with confusion, "Partner, where are we going?"

Uncle Iyer brushed the sweat under his nose and gasped with a smile, "Nothing much, partner."

"Partner, where are we going?"

He stopped the car in the middle of the road, being annoyed. He gulped, "We...We...are lost."

"What!"

He disappointingly nodded and said, "Yup, we are lost."

Kabir turned desperate and queried, "So now what, partner?"

He gasped, "Let's see. Hope for the best." Uncle Iyer leaned back and thought for an idea, but it was meaningless. Also, there was no one to ask for. It was a clean, plane land with greenery all around. No cars, no men, nothing. The car with two passengers stood all alone on that lonely road.

Suddenly, Kabir thought of an idea. He asked Iyer's cell phone, which he gave but was a bit confused.

Kabir immediately looked for signal network for the cell phone reception. And there it was, a good network, and he glimpsed at his partner and said, "Here we are."

Kabir showed their location on Google Maps. Iyer's eyes widened and took the phone crazily. He looked at Kabir with shyness and coughed. "Good. I was also thinking of that." Although Kabir won the situation being smart to anticipate, Uncle Iyer didn't want to lose his ancient pride. He followed the map and found that they were in Yeola, near Nashik. He soon calculated the distance: around 211 km. He swallowed out of hesitance. He gave the phone to Kabir and gripped his hands over the steering wheel. Kabir looked at his face and said, "So, partner, how far we are?"

Iyer just wanted to hide the information, so he just chilled out and said, "Don't worry. We are near."

Anyway, Iyer drove the car towards Pune. The weather was bad. They experienced an energy-sapping heat from the entire surrounding that gave deadly smoke out of the ground. The surface of the road rippled in heat mirages, and they were the lone car in the road to proceed towards the city. Soon this sortie became an odyssey, and Kabir realised it.

CHAPTER 6

After such a happy expected journey, they finally reached Pune, and it was an awful weather. The hot air blew dust and gave them scorching effect. But Kabir was passion enough to keep himself cool. He examined the whole arena and gave a 360-degree look circling the area. His eyes spot-fixed on a green billboard with words *Welcome to Pune*.

He was joyful but remained calm due to the intense heat. He sat back and said, "Partner, we are in Pune. Now let's go to the Histo Library. It's 4:15 pm, and she would reach there around 5:20 pm. So, I don't want to be late."

Uncle Iyer accelerated and zoomed through the entire stretch of the road to finally arrive at the library. It was the worst driving experience Iyer had had in his entire life. He patted in his own shoulder after such a long drive saying "Good revenge."

He removed his specs and took the handkerchief and wiped the sweat off his face, and said with a blurring vision, "Kabir—I mean, partner, just go and ask when she will come."

He heard no reply, so he put his specs again and looked for Kabir. But Kabir was nowhere to be seen. "Hey, Kabir?" he screamed like a fool and at last saw Kabir. He had already been inside the library and was talking to the shopkeeper. Iyer simpered and gasped, "Smart boy."

Kabir got the information about her arrival and read the time on his watch. It was already 5:30 pm. Kabir waited for five more minutes and said to Iyer, "Partner, come. You would've exhausted from the heat inside that car."

Now, Kabir got a companion who can tolerate his talk. They both were comfortable inside the library, waiting for Meera Sharma. Kabir's watch showed six. He became intolerant and started panting. It's really irritating when you wait for someone and don't even know to wait or not because you don't know how important the person is in your life. It was a bitter experience for Kabir. The time was already 8:00 pm. He went and asked the manager, "Sir, today, Meera Sharma was having her book launch here. It's been eight and… and she hasn't come yet."

The manager said in his tired voice, "Beta, the book launch has been cancelled."

"What!" He had a shocking reaction rather than a questionable one.

"I...I mean, how? I mean, why?"

The manager was uninterested in talking to a 16-year-old teen, so he said, "Hmm...May be due to bad weather, she didn't come." The manager made some wild guess for her absence.

Kabir's face turned red in anger and looked like a fish that was drowning to death. He gulped back his tears and motioned outside the library, looking straight and hopeless. Iyer, who was their waiting inside, observed Kabir. "Hey, partner, where are you going?" He stood from the chair and followed him. But Kabir was on his own confused world. Iyer walked past him and grabbed his left hand forcefully. Kabir had lost all his hope and looked tired. He sneered and sniffed. It was really hard for him to bear such a heavy soul-hitting hurt. Iyer shook his body and asked, "Hey, Kabir. What happened?"

"Hey, Kabir. Are you okay?"

"It's the dumbest question. When someone is not feeling good, you ask, 'Are you okay?'."

Kabir was distressed as his face showed clear disappointment, and he closed his eyes, and tears rolled down his face, and he then said, "She...she cheated me." He couldn't even utter a word, as he was choking out of suffocation that he was feeling deep in his heart. He was bleary-eyed, and Iyer became morose.

Iyer couldn't control his emotions, but he tried to and yelled, "Kabir, stop. It's okay. It happens." He then took Kabir's face in his palm and wiped the tears flowing down his cheeks. Iyer said with a sense of inspiration in his eyes, "Hey, partner. Everything is going to be all right. I know you can make it. Do you trust me?" He now stretched his hand to make him promise.

Kabir sniffled and said with broken words. "I trust...y...you," and he put his hand over his palm and promised.

After gaining hope, Iyer said, "Feeling good? Now, we are going to have our dinner. Let's go now." And Iyer went outside, sat in the car and revved the engine. Kabir took the seat and gasped. He was still thinking about Meera Sharma all through the journey. More than a meeting, it now became a challenge for him to meet her.

Then he exhaled and took an oath. With all his effort, he confessed to his destiny, "Partner?"

Iyer looked at him.

"I want to be a writer!"

He felt a flutter in the fit of his stomach as sweat trickled over his face. He said, "Are you joking? You are only 16. So small. It's a tough job, partner." Uncle Iyer put his best foot forward to change his mind.

"Yup!" His nose had reddened, and he yelled, "You told me that I can make it. And through this,

I had made it. And writing a novel is just like writing your feelings and imagination. So, partner, is it a tough work to write your feelings?' Kabir questioned him seriously.

Uncle Iyer thought, *Books have really changed his language and ideas.*

He finally asked him about his opinion. "So, partner, what you really want to be?"

"I want to be a writer."

His eyebrows stretched up seeing his confidence and tenacity.

"Ar…Are you serious?" Uncle Iyer tried to ask him with solemnity.

"As serious as I was the last time during my examination."

His mind-blowing words perplexed Uncle Iyer's mind. On seeing his earnest eyes, Iyer was shocked on the one hand but was happy on the other.

Uncle Iyer made up his wobbly mind and said gently, "Kabir, listen. I know you like her books, and you're extremely passionate and want to meet her. But just think of the situation. You are too small, and I know you very well. So, about writing and novel, please stop dreaming."

He paused and, with an inspiring and confident tone, said, "Partner, it was a dream, but now it's a desire."

CHAPTER 7

Kabir and Iyer returned home—one with a doubtful heart and another with a confident mind.

Doing something great makes you feel good but thinking of getting it done makes you feel better. Kabir's dream obviously became his desire. And his commitment to achieve his desire is unbreakable for sure.

He started reading novels of other authors and struggled in understanding their voice and writing style. He read every genre of books—romance, thriller, action, science fiction, historical fiction, mystery, and almost everything and anything under the sun—to get a spark for his writing. It broadened his imaginative skills. But he found himself helpless without any story to begin his novels; crushed papers were found all through his room—in the dustbin, on the floors, on his bag, table, everywhere. It was quite a disturbing and challenging phase for him.

Witnessing this from a distance, Uncle Iyer felt nostalgic.

That day, Iyer pleaded, "Hey, partner, let's go for a ride. Reading for so long would have tensed up your mind. Outside, just feel the fresh air to relax yourself."

"Who told you I'm bored or tensed, eh? Instead, I'm really enjoying a lot with my new book," countered Kabir, showing the new book cover. Uncle Iyer was quite upset with his changed behaviour and attitude.

Although he is his partner, Uncle Iyer said in a disappointing voice, biting his lips, "Oh…Okay. Carry on."

On another occasion—a holiday—Uncle Iyer, with his trademark smile and in good spirits, entered Kabir's room and said, "Hey, partner. Let's have a match. This time your Roger is going to be finished." Uncle Iyer challenged him enthusiastically. But Kabir was still busy with his new book.

"Sorry, partner, not now. I'm busy." Kabir rejected him and annoyed his uncle once more.

But Uncle Iyer, being a tough guy, said in a slightly harsh tone, "Not again. It's the twelfth time you are rejecting me. For a week I'm observing you, you have become so busy that you don't have time for others. Wow!"

Kabir was still busy with his novel, ignoring him just like an empty glass around the corner.

His remark provoked Iyer, so he snatched the book to seek his attention and said, "Listen, partner, I am leaving in just two days. If you want to be busy with that stuff, then be there. I will not disturb you anymore."

Kabir was still preoccupied with the book than with his partner's words. "Give me my book, partner. I told you, not now."

Uncle Iyer was disappointed. He just wanted to throw that book and cry. But he reassured himself and gave that book to him and said deliberately, "Partner, you have changed." And Iyer left the room with a disheartened soul.

Kabir had turned himself into a bookworm. He was accessing the Internet daily in search of new books and stories.

As day and night, he was seen with a book in his hand, all of them worried about him.

"Hey, Son, you are having your board exams next month. Don't you know? Go and read. Stop wasting your time on such things," his dad insisted him. But Kabir was stuck to his novels like a leech, sucking the stories from it. It was no struggle for Kabir; in fact, he was greatly enjoying his time with books. But on the other side, Uncle Iyer was saddened by such a change in Kabir's behaviour.

Even though Iyer was calm and collected, he'd a stressful mind, so he went to Kabir's room in his absence, silently and secretly, and relived his memories with Kabir by touching the walls and Kabir's things.

The echo of Kabir's laughter filled his mind and felt the essence of his past lives with his small partner.

Seeing himself with his partner on the wall photo, rekindled his memory, *Hey, Kabir, not that way, it's deep. Ha-ha. Partner, catch me. Hahahah...*

Uncle Iyer's eyes now welled up. He removed his glasses and controlled his tears.

"It's my fault." He's torn to pieces. But confidently, he recollected his emotions and stabled himself, as he was a 46-year-old experienced man.

It was the last day in the house before he left, but it was a last for him for so many other reasons. The entire night went out like a whole year. But he never lost the feel and care for Kabir.

In the morning, Uncle Iyer was ready to board his flight, but Kabir was still in deep sleep, courtesy of last night's reading.

Uncle went to his room silently. He saw Kabir lying on his bed in a deep slumber. He touched his face and whispered, "Partner, I need to go. Goodbye."

With no reaction from Kabir, he sighed and kissed his forehead without disturbing his sleep. He then went through the pictures and revisited the memories of them. It proved to be a great stay for Uncle. He had been there many a times, but this time it was quite awful. He then remembered the letter he had scribbled to his partner in a piece of paper the previous night and took it from his pocket. He then placed that paper in the last page of his new book and signed out.

CHAPTER 8

Kabir went to school, without being affected by his partner's leaving.

During the tiffin break, he took out his new novel, which he had just started, and skimmed through the pages. His school bag contained full of novels instead of maths and science books. On observing this, Krish was startled. He went near him and said with a laugh, "Hey, bookish Romeo, is everything okay?"

But Kabir averted his eyes at the sight of Krish and said, "Yup, I'm fine."

"Okay, let's have our bread." There was no reply to his statement. Krish saw him murmur with his lip movements. He lowered down to his bench and said gently, "Okay, Kabir. Take your food. That's all for today."

Still his mind was occupied with silence as Kabir was slightly disturbed.

I think he might have forgotten to bring his stuff, Krish thought. "Bob, c'mon let's share." Bob, being busy with girl's share, was calm.

Being a caring friend, Krish took his tiffin box and offered Kabir. "Kabir, here. I've brought sandwiches. Have it, you'll surely like it."

Kabir was still busy with his reading and said rudely, "No, thanks. I'm good."

Kabir's behaviour annoyed Krish, but being a bestie, Krish neared him with his box and again offered him, saying, "Please, Kabir, for me once." It infuriated Kabir, and he threw his tiffin box with a thud, all the sandwiches now on the floor, soiled. "Don't you get that. I don't want."

Everybody around him was stunned by his action. For a minute, Krish didn't know how to react, his eyebrows stretched and his mind went blank. He couldn't decide what to say. He just lowered his head as he was close to tears and whispered, "Kabir, you've changed." He soon left the place, reflecting the bad behaviour to Kabir. On the other hand, Kabir was nonetheless disturbed by his words. After so much of disrespect he had earned, the only question that was in his mind was "Where is that bloody climax?"

The school was over and Kabir went to his home with hardly any provocation, still with his new book in his hand, *The Harbingers of Happiness*. He put his bag down and looked in the mirror. His eyes searched for a figure with naughty eyes. He stood near the mirror looking at his jaw and whispered, *Kabir, have you really changed?* He stared at the mirror and took a sudden breath. Stepping away from the mirror, he just observed one thing that tickled his mind. It was the stuff his hand was holding—the book.

He focussed his eyes on the book, looking over the book cover.

Then, he placed the book on his bed and looked himself again on the mirror. And this time he felt the change. He was bare-handed. A sweet smile crossed through his face as he explored his happiness. *Kabir, now there you are. I got it. Uncle Iyer and Krish are just feeling jealous of your passion. You should read more books.*

After a slight pause, *Ya. You should.*

He changed his clothes, freshened up, and had his lunch, and in the afternoon, he was occupied with his book, once again.

At twilight, when Mom was busy making coffee, Uncle Iyer called from USA.

"Hello, Iyer."

"Hello," he answered gently.

"So, how are you?" Mom questioned him, to know about his health and doings.

"Of course, fine here. But the weather is not. What's going around there?"

Both of them exchanged their pleasantries. Then, Mom remembered about Kabir and said, "Are you not going to talk to your partner?"

Uncle sighed. He felt lonelier. He became dull and gasped, "Hmm...He would be busy. I will call you later." His lowered voice puzzled her, and she then said suddenly, "No, I must call Kabir. He might be free, and your mind will be stress-free after talking with him."

Uncle Iyer thought of replying in negative, but he confronted and said in a low voice, "Sure."

"Kabir, it's your partner on the phone," Mom shouted from the ground floor.

On hearing his mom's faint voice shouting, he yelled, "Mommm...I'm busy." Hearing his reply, she thought, *where you have time for anyone else?*

"Uncle, you're right, he is busy." Listening to her statement, he felt desperate and ended the call.

Keeping the phone receiver angrily, Kabir's mom hurried towards his room, only to find him lying on the bed with a book in his hand. She was disgusted by his behaviour. "Kabir, you should have time for others and especially for your partner. But you. Leave it. You are not going to listen to anybody." And she left the room furiously closing the door hard.

Kabir was distressed by the comments from his family and friends. *Everybody is saying something. What wrong have I done?* he thought, and he gave couple of days rest for his book reading.

INTERVIEW

Kabir giggled with a sigh. He looked at her and gulped, "Have you ever made yourself look foolish among others?"

The interviewer laughed and said, "Ya, many a times."

"Good, but not like me."

Kabir looked depressed and sipped another cup of his coffee.

He brimmed with confidence and said, "I was becoming not what I was. I...I became the stickler for my books. I couldn't find myself in that bookish crowd. I left my partner annoyingly and he left me unknowingly. But you know what? Life teaches us the right thing at the very wrong time. And... And...it happened...

CHAPTER 9

Kabir tried to make good use of his day in school, but he felt a kinda pain surrounding him like a bad omen. In school, the teachers were busy and active, because of the upcoming board exams, whereas the students were lazy and undisciplined.

Kabir reached his home, feeling tired and reckless, with his bag in his shoulder. *Oh! Such an awful day,* he thought. When he entered the home, a kind of deadly silence surrounded him. For a while, he thought of something but soon returned to present status. He then slipped through the entrance and slowly proceeded towards his room. While crossing over the dinning space, his eyes stuck to his mother who was crying at that moment.

He tried to reason out the cause of his mother's crying but failed to succeed. It was a kind of desolate sobbing that comes from a person drained of all hope. Kabir then paced towards her and put the bag down.

He gently waved towards her and asked, "Mom, tell me what happened?"

Dad was standing near her, busy with phone calls, as if it's a great emergency. Kabir just called his mother and said, "Hey, Mom. What happened?"

She was speechless, and the answer was uncertain. Kabir immediately talked to his father. "Dad, what's going on?"

But his father was unresponsive. Kabir became intolerant and cried out, "Is there anybody who can tell me what's the matter?"

Mom cleared her eyes and pulled Kabir gently towards her. She waved her smooth palm over his head and said with her promising eyes, "Son…" She inhaled some air to steady herself.

On the other hand, Kabir was uncontrollable and intolerant, as his eagerness to know what happened skyrocketed. His eyes reddened, with little tears trickling through his cheeks. He then shouted with a little force, "Hey, Mom. What happened? Please, Dad. Tell…What's happening."

And he screamed, "Mom, please. Pleaseee…!"

Mom then said in a spur of a moment as she burst out, "Your uncle had met with an accident!" And she was torn to pieces with this message. It's a great shock to Kabir's ears, like when someone realises that he is walking with bare legs over spiky glass pieces resting on burnt coal.

Kabir fell on the sofa like a heavy metal. He sat silently, feeling despaired. His ears can indeed hear the shouting of his inner mind. The stabled posture grew morose with every second of silence. The wistful look on his face was clearly visible.

Mom moaned, "Kabir…"

She paused for a moment, and with every word, she stiffened her eyes to control her tears. "It was a bad weather, and…the roads were slippery. And your uncle was just…crossing the road…and…and…

"And an inexperienced driver, unmindfully racing, slammed brakes upon the slippery road, and…and…

"skid on the road. He lost…the control…and…and…it hit…your uncle." And Mom cried for the moon.

The tears raced through the cheeks of Kabir and made him to lament.

"And now…now…he is in…coo…coma, and…and the doctors don't know how much time it will take?" said Mom woefully. Summer's heat was making the situation even more hotter.

Every word his mother uttered was like a nail piercing his flesh.

"It's nottt… It's not fair…" he said in his choked voice. He looked upon the ceiling to control his tears. Soon he hurried to his upstairs room.

He fell on his bed and burst out once again. *No, it can't be*. He nodded with a warm and moist voice. His grief was uncontrollable, tightening his chest. He just lost everything. It just seemed like the walls, the table, and everything in the house were pointing and blaming him for this accident. A kinda of eerie silence occupied his head.

He calmed himself for a second to clear his mind that was in dilemma. Coursing over the room, he looked at his book shelf with a collection of books. He gasped and took out his new book. His hands perused the book cover gently, thinking of his beloved partner.

It's my fault… Yup, it's mine. In the time of searching new books, I lost my partner. If I had talked to him, it would be pleasure for me. But being a selfish, I rejected him.

He nodded and thought, *everybody was right. I…I…I have changed. What I have been, I don't know. But…but because of this change, I am without my partner.*

"I'm sorry partner!" he howled. Then, he controlled himself.

It's just because of these books. He took all the books and threw them on the floor. He unexpectedly discovered a piece of paper pressing outside from his new book. *What's that?*

Kabir took that piece of paper from the book, unfolded it and read with complete focus.

CHAPTER 10

Dear Partner,

So, finally, you are going to listen to me, through this letter. I'm proud of you, at the same time may be not. You might not like it, or you would be busy, but take a bit and think, of course, about me, or for your partner.

Every day is a new day, a new path to walk, a new drink to drink, a new talk to talk, a new thought to think, but mostly it's a matter of a new life to live. But more interestingly, all these are quite related to each other. It means that your living depends upon how you walk, how you drink, how you talk and how you think. You might be pertaining to think, is your partner become a loon? *I know it's a bad joke.*

I'm not going to argue with you, partner. But you have changed. Not more what you are but pertaining to be like it. You are like that water, which have become ice, but forgotten that inside it you have left so many pores. But as a partner I forgive you not for your unchangeable past, but for your bright future.

Your fancy faith upon your burning desire is going to rock. Partner, I trust you that you can be a writer. Your thirst is all on your eyes. I felt it. However, it just needs some direction.

You may be pathless, helpless, careless, although remember I will always be with you as an old partner. And of course, I'm just leaving you without being informing you. But still, your partner will always be remembered by you. Always. And the day is not so far, my partner, when your authentic writer Miss Meera Sharma would come to meet you. Be ready!

And one more thing, the next time when I come, be ready with your Roger. I will not pay mercy. Okay.

Yours old Partner

Uncle Iyer

CHAPTER 11

Kabir's hands fluttered and shivered with instant nervousness. With regret and grief, he shed tears and sweat. Kabir lamented for his beloved partner. He held the letter with utmost pain as his salty drops of tears dripped and wetted the floor.

I'm so...sorry, partner. He inhaled the air agonisingly.

I should have listened to...to you, my partner.

You always meant a lot to me, always. I'm really sorry, partner. He controlled his teary eyes and drifted his legs slowly. He then realised the books were scattered on the floor. He took one of the books and quarrelled, *It's all because of these books.* He cried out and placed the book very hard. He then lay on the bed with wet eyes and slept for hours, sobbing.

The darkness had rained and it departed. And the sun shined the next day peacefully.

Kabir woke, his eyes looking tired. He yawned, and no doubt, he realised that he had slept too long. His eyes scanned the room and found nothing interesting except for those scattered books. The world around him that day seemed very bright, as the yellow beam of sunlight scattered through the windows, and Kabir felt light.

He drowsily walked slowly downstairs, keeping every footstep carefully. He looked at his face on the bathroom mirror. He still felt the intense pain through his reddened eyes. He then splashed the water and relaxed himself. It was a Sunday morning, and the clock had just struck ten. So Kabir dressed up well and sat silently in his room. He tried to tidy up his room, but the guilt bothered him to sit alone. So, without any provocation Kabir laid on the bed and looked at the ceiling.

"Hmm…" He inhaled deeply to calm himself. He closed his eyes for a minute to relax his body. Suddenly some random images flicked through his mind in a rush, but he couldn't decide what the images were and tried to escape from the dilemma he was having. Instantly, he woke up, stood right and breathed rapidly, swallowing.

Soon flood of tears rushed through his eyes. Some unknowing pain followed his chest unceasingly, making his body shiver.

*Partner, I am sorry…*he sobbed, his palms holding the floor tightly. The tears wetted the floor. All of a sudden, Kabir heard a faint voice outside. He looked through the window and saw Krish waiting for him with his bicycle.

"Hey, Kabir, let's go and play. You haven't played for a long time. Let's play. And may your mind gonna be okay," Krish insisted him.

Bob, standing beside Krish, grumbled, "Kab, you might haven't slept, so you just take rest. Okay?"

Kabir shuddered for a second, wiped his eyes from tears and replied in a low voice, "No. Coming."

Kabir went out without his cycle and walked to the field with his tired and thoughtful mind. Seeing all his friends playing and enjoying the game, he became uneasy. So, he searched for a better place and found one—a wooden bench under the shade of a big apple tree. He sat comfortably on the bench.

The sun light that was poring through the leaves of the tree was dim and felt good and right for Kabir. "Oh, God!" Kabir sighed.

He just closed his eyes, when he heard an old, experienced voice disturbing him. "For whom are you going to feel so much low, my son?"

Kabir looked right above his head and saw an old man with a hat and greybeard. The map of the wrinkles on his face described most of his incredible journeys. The old man sat beside him, taking his hat off, and asked Kabir, "My son, what happened? You are not playing with them."

Kabir gasped, "Hmm. My name is Kabir."

"Don't ask mine, it's horrible. But you can call me 'partner'. It sounds good."

He was happy to hear that word once again, and he uttered with a confusing voice, deliberately, "Ya. I mean, yup. Sure."

The old man was little bit confused with his behaviour and reminded him about the question he asked earlier. "So, Kabir, you haven't answered my question."

Kabir became little bit nervous, but answered, "Hmm…nothing much, just simply watching." The old man captured his mood, and clearing his throat, lifting his body back slightly, he spoke, "My son was a great student, a topper. He was in IIT, in his last year. He was doing good. But soon what happened with him, I…I don't know. He would always wake up at 4:00 am to study, but that day was different. His friends heard no alarm and knocked his room's door to check. But he didn't respond. His loving friends went out without a second thought. The whole day he was missing—in the college, in the campus, in the canteen; he was nowhere. The next day, all the teachers with the students waited in front of his room, and finally, they had to break into his room. What they saw was painful. My son was hanging in the fan. He committed suicide. There was a suicide note that read 'I'm out of this evil games'."

"They called me, and I remember, I was gardening. I never thought of that. My wife still believes he is alive and asks me for his return. How easy it is…"

The old man with a heavy heart look towards the sky and paused for a moment. He then realised and rubbed his tear-filled eyes.

He gasped, "But now it's okay. Because I learned that life is ever moving. It never stops for you nor for anybody, neither long nor short. It is even throughout this lively universe."

The old man took a deep breath and looked upon the blue sky. Kabir was fascinated and said, "You are really a strong old man."

The old man with a glint of smile said, "What about you, Kabir?" Instantly, a red ball came across the seat, rolling.

"Kabir, pass it." Kabir just heard the request and took the ball and passed it to them. Kabir was bit confused by the question. He sat and replied to the old man's query, "Nothing, partner. I just feel, I am just feeling lonely."

"It means you have lost the one who make you feel contented," the old man said. Kabir was reminded again of his dear partner and became cheerless. Then the old man put his hands over Kabir's shoulder and said, "Kabir, you know what? When I realised about his absence, I really felt bad. But the time I accepted that, no, he is with me always, near me, I really felt something good."

"Life is like a lake, still and silent. So always it seems to be perfect and good. But the time anyone throws a stone, our life becomes disturbed and troubled. The ripples make problems and chaos. Instead of pushing or trying hard to free ourselves, we must stand and wait. Because with the course of time, the ripples become lighter and lighter so is our problems. And finally, we will be living the same life as like the still and silent lake but with or without somebody special."

Kabir felt his heart fulfilled and felt contented. He understood the essence of happiness and smiled, closing his eyes and feeling the soft winds with every heartbeat.

Kabir said with a smile, "Thanks, partner."

"You're welcome."

Kabir then uttered, "But...But I have already a partner. So, I can't call you as my partner."

The old man looked a bit confused. He smiled and said, "All right. You can call me as your second partner."

Kabir grimaced, "Okay. Once again, second partner, thanks a lot."

And the old man left the place without his knowing, giving a source of light to Kabir. Kabir looking at the sky confidently and said, *Uncle Iyer, you will always be here, with me, with your tiny partner.*

Kabir went to home with aspiration and hope. His second partner made his heart and mind stay peaceful. The day was about to end, and he, with his room full of memories, completed his day off. He lay on his bed, switched off the lights and hoped for a better tomorrow, saying, "Good night, partner."

The next day was fantastic, joyful and wonderful. Kabir switched off the alarm, slipped through the bedsheets and then through the stairs. He looked in the mirror and gazed, saying, *Kabir, you are going to make your day great. So, let's start the game.*

He brushed through his white walls of his room, singing joyfully. He took bath, hearing melody songs. His mother was quite happy to see the change in Kabir. She made a good breakfast. "Good morning, Mom. Waoo! Looks delicious!" Kabir took his bag, enjoyed his breakfast and went to the school in his bicycle. In the school, he was glad to meet Krish and Bob, and wished them good morning. And they had a great meeting over a new girl who had come to the city. Everything went well with the teachers and studies.

Kabir nurtured the essence of goodness in all, and it's the best of both worlds.

CHAPTER 12

Kabir was back in his home after completing the practice at school. From the next day their board exam was beginning, and he was confident of acing every subject.

When he reached home, he found a suitcase at the front door. "Mom, who has come?"

"No one has come. We're leaving," Mom replied, carrying his vanity bag.

Kabir was astonished, and he asked in a surprise mood, "'We?' What does it mean? I'm not going anywhere. From tomorrow I'm having my exams. Sorry, Mom, I can't."

"I know. That's why we are leaving you here. Only your father and I are going."

Kabir realised the problem, so he acted, "Mom! How can you leave such a small child here at home, all alone?"

"Ohh! I know your drama, stop it. You are not going to live alone. I've talked to the neighbour about this, and you are going to stay there until we come."

Kabir was awe struck listening to his neighbour; he remembered the incident when he was scolded by that old aunt when he broke one of their windows while playing. "N-o-o, it's too horrible."

"No excuses, Son." Mom was on her way to leave the house with the luggage, and then the father came, playing with his keys.

"Papa, where you and Mom are going actually?"

Father looked surprised and said, "Hmm....we are going to USA to see Uncle Iyer."

Kabir was silent, but not sad. He lowered his voice and said softly, "Ohh...to see my partner." Being a concerned father, he went nearer to him, sat down and said, holding his hands, "Hmm... It's really hard to live alone without parents, but believe me, living alone has some joy in itself. Take care, my son." He patted his shoulder and proceeded towards the parkway.

Kabir was slightly hurt by the happenings, but being a brave and talented boy, he believed in his faith and destiny.

The car motioned near the driveway and honked the horn. The Mother hurried with her so-called luggage and vanity bag and kissed Kabir's forehead, giving her heart felt love, and said, "Son, we will come soon. Take care."

She sat in the car and waved at him. Kabir acknowledged, "Love you, Dad and Mom."

"See you."

Kabir was tired, so he went inside the house. He removed his bag and had lunch, as Mom had already prepared for him. While taking his lunch, he thought for a second about his neighbour. *It's going to be too much torturing to live there. It's better that I should live on the streets than to live in that old lioness den.*

He sighed and napped for a while. He thought of those things he did last time when he was confronted by that old women.

The day after, he had his exam. He woke up early in the morning and sincerely revised all chapters.

INTERVIEW

"Exams are really profitable only when we score good marks."

The interviewer smiled and said, "Ya, sure."

"And…And, my friends, they are really good for nothing. They will ask me like 'Kabir, which exam do we have today?' I mean who'll do these? I mean how such friends exist? I still doubt."

She giggled and said, "Damn right."

She thought for a second and asked, "By the way, did you go there?"

"Truly not. I was not at all in the mood to face her approach. But my mom. Ah! …

CHAPTER 13

Kabir locked the house and went to the school to write his exam. Three hours went silently in the school. Some were talented in sincerely scanning others' answer sheet. And friends were ready to help them. Some were busy in writing 'Om' and some in search of answers. In the whole class Kabir was the bright spot. He was calm and contended. He completed the paper and gave it to the invigilator. "Good, Kabir," muttered his madam.

"Thank you, mam," Kabir replied. On his way to home, his mind was filled with thoughts. "Hmm...Hmm...Hm...Ya...No...Hm..." Well, nobody knows about him. He wandered around his home and howled. "Mom, I am home." For a second, he had already forgotten about their departure. He whispered, "Oops! Sorry!" While he was busy removing his shoes, he heard the phone ring. He hurried to the room upstairs and picked the phone, and he raised and squeaked, "Hello."

"Hello, Son."

Kabir urged swiftly, "How is my uncle? Is he all right? What the doctors are saying?"

Mother just held up the call and said, "Have patience. He is all right, but he is still in coma."

"Wow! How can anybody be all right being in coma?" Kabir sighed.

"By the way, I just talked to Mrs Kanta. And what I found was you haven't been to their house yesterday. Can I know the reason, Mr Kabir?" Mother joked.

Kabir added with a smile, "Oh! That's just… Ahh…Leave it, Mom. I'm not going to live there. She is quite terrible like a witch."

"Don't be rude, Kabir. I've talked to her in the morning and you are going to take lunch there. No more excuses. So, how's your exam?"

"Oh…It was fantastic," Kabir giggled.

"Hmm…Good to hear that. Okay, pack up the things you need, and remember, you must lock the doors."

"And one more thing, take bath and go, okay?"

He whispered, "It's all in their genes."

"What!"

"Bye."

Kabir still had a different plan for the day. Krish and Bob came to his house and the war began. Three of them, being connected through their joysticks and garlic bread, played against the clock.

Krish acted, "Roger, you are gone."

And Kabir started dwelling on the past. He suddenly left the place and went outside in search of a mood changer.

"I'm just coming."

Going through the field, he sat down at his place under that big apple tree. And he exhaled. Being busy with cricket, the field was full of people with their children, most of the time. And Kabir remembered an incident with his partner. When they were playing football, his partner had hit him quite hard on his face that he couldn't go to school the next day.

And suddenly, a ball rushed towards him, and he being in a really bad mood threw the ball out of the field.

"Hey!" he heard a girly voice and became attentive and left the place.

CHAPTER 14

Kabir had a bad attitude towards Mrs Kanta. But still, he had to make his clothes fit in his travelling bag, informally. And made himself ready to face off.

Carrying his bag on his shoulders, he was in front of his neighbour's door. For the last time, he prayed once and murmured, "Oh God, help me."

He knocked the door, and with a steady mind, he followed the rules. *No, Kabir. Be gentle. Use the calling bell.*

He cooled himself, flicked his fingers for a second and pressed the doorbell. After a minute, the door was at its place and he noticed that the door was open. With all his might and main, he pushed the door; it seemed weird. The hall way was dark; the sun light came from the door's slit. Behind Kabir's body, a long shadow ensued. For Kabir, it was like going inside the Niagara Falls. With this mindset, he motioned inside, slowly and safely, like a Russian spy submarine. Kabir muttered, *Oh, Kabir. You are going good!*

At halfway mark, he observed the light coming from the entrance of another door. It was like getting a four-leafed clover in a bunch of odds. Kabir was fine with his walk and moved nearer with every inch. He gaped inside the room through the corridor, left and right. And suddenly, a heavy paint roller hit his head hard. Kabir sneered with pain, "Awhh...Who's that?"

Kabir looked upward and there stood a girl. She was quite gorgeous and impressive. Kabir had already been bowled by her naughty eyes and breath-taking facial expressions. She was standing on a stepladder, struggling with her long and smooth hair. For Kabir, the time had stopped for a moment and he blushed.

She greeted, "Hello. You Kabir, right?"

Her voice is so sweet, Kabir thought. He was just looking at her dumbfounded.

She waved her hand over his face, stating, "Kabir, are you all right?"

Kabir gulped as he was distracted. "Ya...Ya...I am...I am all right."

"Hmm...Good. My name is Tara." She stretched her hand towards him for a handshake. "Myself, Kabir." Their hands pressed against each other.

"Ya, I know. Aunt has already told me that a bad guy is coming here from the neighbourhood."

Kabir coughed, "And...And what else she claimed?"

"Much more. But leave it, I am just busy in colouring this wall. And really sorry for that." She pointed towards his head.

Kabir ignored that one and confessed, "No, It's okay." Tara smiled, and Kabir was fascinated by her behaviour.

The brush that hit his head was lying on the floor, dripping with paint on the floor. "Ohh... Kabir. Pass that paintbrush, and can you please hold the bucket till I complete it?"

Kabir was ready to fulfil her request and held the bucket. If she had told him to hold it for a lifetime, he'd have readily agreed.

She was dipping each time she took the brush to the wall, and it was quite horrible to see her painting. She was really a bad painter. While brushing over the wall, she mentioned, "You know what, Kabir? Painting is just great. It's really hard to do it, but you see, I'm fine in it. If you want, I can teach you."

Kabir was startled. *Is she giving a suggestion to a national-level competitor?* he thought and smiled.

"No thanks, Tara. It's fine. By the way, I never saw you here," Kabir pleaded.

"But, bad luck, I have seen you."

"I mean where?"

"Yesterday, you threw the ball out without any reason and even didn't respond. Cool."

"Oh! That's called frustration in the real sense."

"Cool. Actually, I'm from Chandigarh. But I have come here for holidays."

Kabir raised his eyebrows showing a sense of confusion with goodness. "Hm. Cool," he murmured.

"Stop flirting. Okay?"

The brush gave up its colours with every stroke, and being a waiter, Kabir held the bucket. *She is so pretty and cute*, Kabir blushed. It was quite breath-taking, but still he was staring at her like cattle. "So, today, you were having your test. How's it?"

For a second, Kabir focussed on her query, then her looks and replied, "Ya, it was fantastic."

"Cool."

Time went out with every stroke and dip. They had a couple of good talks, and finally, it was over. She waved with satisfaction, and Kabir, being confused, looked at the wall to control his laughter.

"It's over. How is it, Kabir?"

Kabir scratched his head and looked at the wall. He was just looking for some adjectives to falsely beautify her lousy painting. He swallowed and uttered, "It's...It's really brilliant, mind-blowing, stunning, shinning, lovely. It's just extraordinary." And looked at her.

Since he was overexaggerating, Tara suspected his praising. She looked at him surprisingly and said, "Hmm. It was too much. It means you don't know anything about painting. Cool."

"You are smarter than your art."

Both the teen went out of that room, giving some rest to the wall. Tara was washing her hands, and Kabir, being hypnotised, was staring at her.

"Stop looking like that," she grumbled.

"Oh. I'm sorry."

She cleaned her hands, and both of them heard Mrs Kanta's shouting, "Hey, Tara, just come and have your lunch right now."

She looked at Kabir and yelled, "Yes, Aunt, coming."

She asked Kabir to join the lunch too. The pair sat on the chairs for lunch. Mrs Kanta looked narrowly with her piped eyes while serving to Kabir. And he, being fearful, swallowed each morsel with fear and comforted himself.

Kabir, in order to break the silence and monotony, joked, showing up his acting talent, "Aunt, it's really delicious, superb, nice."

But once again his over exaggeration brought untoward problem to him. She looked carefully, narrowed her eyes and stated, "So what? For that delicious, superb and nice food, will you pay for those broken windows?"

Kabir was awestruck and his jaw dropped. He was just annoyed by her comment, although lunch was over with uneasiness.

CHAPTER 15

Ohh...It was really a mess! Is there anyone more dangerous and cruel like her? Kabir was really angry with Mrs Kanta. He headed off to home as it was already five in the evening, and he had his second exam the next day. *Ohh...Shit! Kabir, you have to read throughout the night, man.* He was committed and determined with a purpose and sat on the chair with his books. He was silently revising his chapters.

While the twilight set in, Kabir observed from the windows that Tara going outside with a kit bag in her sports outfit with matching shoes.

He was in dilemma; his one of the two main inner characters, Kabiroh thought, *Hey, Kabir, she is so pretty. You should show your talent in sports. It's the correct time to impress her, bro.*

His other inner character Kabirah thought, *No, Kabir, you must study. Chasing a girl and trying to impress her will waste your time.*

Listening to Kabiroh, he heard, *Stop, you Kabirah. Listen, Kabir, you know that behind every successful man there is a woman. Believe in yourself, okay.*

No, Kabir, don't listen to Kabiroh. You must study. Don't listen him.

No, Kabir, listen.

Nooo.

Kabir was struggling to control his mind. He just shouted loudly, *Stop, you both*. And both disappeared upon his shout.

Kabir inhaled for a second and calmed himself. Looking through the ceiling, he saw Kabiroh whispering, *Kabir, don't lose her. She can be your best friend*. With this thought, he faded.

Kabir got up from his chair and went outside, following Tara. He took a short sprint and squeaked, "Hey, Tara, wait."

Tara heard the voice and saw Kabir panting. He reached near her and said with fluttered words, "Ta…Tara…Where…Where…you…"

Tara cared about Kabir and suggested him, "Control, Kabir. Breathe. Inhale. Cool."

"Ya, Tara, I was just asking, where you are going."

Tara was allured on seeing his interest. "Hmm… I'm just going to the club, for badminton."

Kabir found himself comfortable to hear her answer. "Ohh…badminton, great."

"Don't you know to play badminton?"

Kabir thought for a second and remembered the last time he had played badminton. It had been six months since he had used the racquet. Suddenly, with confusion surrounding, he thought from his left brain, *Kabir, don't worry, just accept it.*

Tara snapped her fingers off, and Kabir was now focussed on Tara. He cleared his throat and coughed, "You know I...I'm a pro in badminton. I have won many trophies. Yet, no one has ever seen me playing."

"Good then, let's go."

Kabir was excited, as he thought to be a partner of Tara, and he would enjoy the moment. But he had barked on the wrong tree.

They reached the club, and Kabir was eager and thrilled. He saw a big space with many courts and players smashing and tossing the shuttles. It was really a busy arena to play.

Tara took out her kitbag and grabbed two racquets. "Kabir, take it. Let's play."

That part of Kabir was known to be excited.

Tara said something to her friend, and she left the court, leaving both to play. Tara was ready on her side, and Kabir went near to her. "Hey, Kabir, just go to the other side."

Kabir was a bit annoyed but thought, *Ohh...She needs some warm up. Good.*

While his excitement level was reaching its zenith, he heard a whooshing sound of racquets coming from the next court, "Kabir, ready. Love all, play."

Kabir just shot back his head and saw Tara in front of her. She was just serving the cork. Seeing it, he interrupted, "Wait. Wait. Tara, I can't play with you."

Tara appealed, "Why?"

Kabir was a bit nervous that time and said, "Actually I don't want you to lose. And my smashes may hurt you. Can't we play doubles?"

Tara chuckled, "Don't be fool, Kabir. I'm not a child, and by the way I am the best here. So, let's start."

Kabir swallowed once and gaped at her. Seeing her tossing the cork, he thought, *she is going to kill me*. And he became anxious. She started the match with her serving, and Kabir being fearful waited for his own response.

"Love all, play."

The cork flew in the air and Kabir had no other choice but to accept it. He somehow reciprocated the cork up with a stroke. The shuttle was a bit up towards the ceiling, and Kabir was staring at the shuttle movement. With a rapid move, Tara took a flight and smashed the shuttle right to Kabir. The shuttle dashed and hit Kabir on his face. It hit very hard on Kabir that he felt the pain, rubbing his nose.

"Ouch. Kabir, are you all right? I'm really sorry."

Being manly, he replied, "It's okay, Tara, I haven't played for months. That's why. But don't you worry, I can handle it."

Kabir showed his acting but got stuck in a bad hole. He tried his best but badly failed. Tara went on smashing, and Kabir was dodging to keep himself on the safer side.

Finally, the score was 21:1. Kabir was badly beaten by her. Tara came near to Kabir running with sweat and victory. "Are you all right?"

Kabir was not in a position to even utter a word. He gave a fake smile to show that he was fine. Tara gleamed and joked, "So, Mr Specialist, I beat you." Tara was happy with it; on the other hand, Kabir had a miserable situation but was contended with Tara's happiness.

Both of them returned home quite tired. Kabir just slept over the bed and saw the clock. It was already nine. *Oh, shit. Kabir, you are finished*. He just jumped from the bed and started reading.

Tara got freshened up, and while drying up her hair, she saw Kabir in his room, studying vigorously. She smiled and left him to study.

CHAPTER 16

Kabir didn't know how he managed to prepare for the exam. After coming from school, being a hot and sultry day, he had lunch and roamed lonely in his room.

He peeked from the windows as the sunlight flashing on him. He was just thinking about his partner. *You will be perfect soon, partner*, he made a silent wish.

"Hey, Kabir," Tara screamed and Kabir got cold feet.

She chuckled at his action, and at the same time, she apologised for her behaviour.

Tara stretched her hand for a handshake with doubt, "Friends?"

Kabir was waiting for that moment. He smiled and shook hands and replied, "Sure. Friends."

Tara is really a good girl, quite friendly and have a mixture of traits, Kabir thought and smiled.

"So, now tell me, who is your partner?" Tara asked him, triggering his past actions. He was confused and quite nervous.

Tara teased him, saying, "I guess it might be your puppy."

Kabir became nostalgic after listening to her stupid predictions. Kabir whooped, "Not at all. I have no dogs. Okay, and I have no girlfriend. And never I had. Okay."

"I didn't ask you."

Tara became judgemental and agreed with him and dared, "So, who's your partner, Kabir?"

Kabir's mouth was twitching, "Oh…No one. Ya, no one. All right."

Tara was not at all satisfied with his reply and knew that he was hiding something. "Kabir, you are really a piece of work and, of course, a bad actor. I'm your friend, you just accepted it. You should tell your friend all about it, shouldn't you?"

Quite clever she is, Kabir thought.

He wanted to leave her query unanswered, but pointing towards his conscience, as a friend, he was bound to tell her all the truth. He took a deep breath and told his sad story that was a mix of happiness, loneliness and depression. But he didn't mention about his dream and desire of becoming a writer. (secret, maybe)

"I don't know how it happened, but it left me shattered."

Listening to his woeful story, Tara had a rush of emotions as she was quite sensitive, and she felt as if a fish out of water. She soon became teary-eyed and endured a grief-stricken pain. But being his friend, she made returned to normalcy and confessed, suggesting, "Hey, Kabir. It's not your fault. And don't cry. Be strong, okay."

Kabir wiped his tear-filled eyes and listened to her suggestions. "Thanks, Tara." Their eyes met, and they were now deeply connected to each other, by sharing their pain and friendship.

On looking at the clock, Tara reminded, "Hey, Kabir, it's going to be seven in the evening. You should now study. It's your last exam, so prepare it well, okay?"

Kabir was happy to have such a great friend who was helpful and shared every bit of his loss and grief by taking part on his painful journey. So, he became focussed on study mode. Tara never interfered while he studied. The moon oscillated and faded soon to bring the morning sunshine.

Next morning, Tara woke up and saw Kabir. She giggled and smiled as he slept on his books while he studied last night. He was sleeping like a small baby, cute and innocent. Tara was quite attracted by his appearance. As a friend, she went out of that room and let him rest and revel in his world of dreams.

"Finally, Kabir. It's over," Bob said, being exhausted.

"Yup. Now I have all the time around for Tara," Kabir said, dreaming.

"Huh? Tara? Who's she?" Krish pointed out. "Ah. That's…That's a new movie released, Trek. What do you say about going there?"

"C'mon, guys, it's our day. We must celebrate. We must go for *Born to Fight*," Bob cheered up.

Kabir walked around and confessed, "We can find a lot of blonde girls out there in the hall, for sure."

"Watching movie is yet another way of celebration. Huh?" Bob modified his statement. Both of them giggled.

"Fine, I will arrange for three tickets," said Krish.

"It would be much better, if you could arrange one more."

"But why?"

"Nothing, I just need it for someone."

They soon disappeared from the school field, and Kabir ran to Tara's house.

After lunch, Kabir went to Tara's room. He saw Tara busily writing with her brittle pen. Being gentle and straightforward, he said, "Let's go, Tara."

"Hey, Hi, Kabir."

"I was just thinking would you like to go for a movie with me."

With her pen on her lips and eyes swaying across the room, she looked at Kabir and said, "Cool. I would really like to go with you."

For Kabir, her seal of approval was like getting an approval appointment from Roger, *Born to Fight.*

"Hey, Kabir, let's go." Both the fellows shouted like the odds, which meant trouble for them. Mrs Kanta came out of the house patio and screamed, "What the hell are you doing here? Can't you just leave the world in peace?"

"Sorry, Aunty. By the way, is Kabir there?"

"He is. Go and take him with you. Hurry up!"

After so much of pleasing, Tara was permitted to watch a movie. "So, she is Tara? Nice. For her, you wanted a special extra-large seat, eh?" Krish giggled.

"I only wanted a flower for my heart to heal my memories," Bob added with his third-class acting.

Kabir wasn't able to slap them in front of her, and Tara wasn't able to slam them with her slangs in front of him. So, both remained silent.

They reached the movie hall on time, and Kabir took the seat beside Tara. That moment, Kabir had butterflies in his stomach, on seeing Tara's face. *She is more beautiful,* he thought. Movie was playing as usual, but Kabir had a different plan. He asked, "So, Tara, do you believe in ghosts?"

Devouring the popcorns around, she said, "Yup. That's why I believe in you."

After her sarcastic reply, Kabir remained silent and looked at the screen like a fool.

"Cool, it was nice. Kabir?" Tara squeaked moving out of the hall.

"Ya, it was fantastic," Kabir lied. Because nobody likes horror movies except girls. Maybe it's all in their genes.

Kabir returned home with Tara, and he was all free, so he called his mom.

"Hello, Mom."

"Kabir! How are you, my son?"

"I'm fine, Mom. What about my partner?"

She uttered, "His condition is improving on a daily basis, but still only a miracle can bring him out of the coma."

Kabir became half hopeful and was happy to hear about his improved condition. For about an hour, he shared his experience with his neighbour.

Kabir kept the phone receiver down and roamed around Tara's room. He just opened the door and found Tara missing. He closed the door and again observed her room. *Her room is just beautiful like her,* he thought. It was clean and tidy, with soothing fragrance of sunlight emanating. Her bookshelves were quite authentic and mesmerised him. Kabir remembered about his hard past. He gasped, "Ohh..."

He saw some incomplete writings sitting at her writing desk. He took it and observed that it was some kind of couplets or short poems. He held the copy, and it was written:

People are so busy in their zone
that they don't care about you and you become alone.
But being alone is not that you are weak,
but strong enough to shine like a gemstone.

Kabir was astonished. *Wow! I didn't know that she likes these things. Good.*

He turned to the next page and read some more:

Inside you just light up that fire,
Because you are the one who can inspire.

Kabir was highly impressed and inspired by her writings. He put down the copy and looked around.

While he wandered his eyes over the various things in her room, he saw an unsolved Rubik's Cube on her study table. *Might she have tried it a lot but failed in it,* he thought.

Unlike in badminton, Kabir was quite exceptional in maths and algorithms. He could solve the cube in less than 10 seconds. So, he held the Cube and looked at it. Suddenly, Tara pushed the door and entered inside. "Ohh, Kabir. Hi." Her hairs were wet with a pink towel.

Kabir just put the Cube down as he didn't want her to know that he touched her belongings. Tara queried, "Can you solve it?"

Kabir was confident with his work, "Yup, sure I can."

Kabir just grabbed the Cube and looked it for a second. And within a flash, he knocked down the cube, fully solved. It was so fast that Tara stood there like a statue, staring at it.

"Wow, Kabir! Cool! It was magnificent. Brilliant. How did you do that?"

Kabir ought to say, "Hmm...It's just a kind of magic my hands do. I just look it first for a few seconds and move it like I'm buttering on its surface."

"It's really a great talent. Everybody should know."

Kabir waited for her reply but he didn't get one. So Kabir coughed and said, "If you don't mind, I can make you do the same as I do."

"Really! Will you teach me, Kabir?"

He became too excited to get such an offer. He had ants in his pants. He accepted it with no second thoughts and shook hands with her, appreciating her interest.

INTERVIEW

"Actually, I mean seriously I can solve a Rubik's Cube."

"I know. That's why I brought a Rubik's Cube with me. Have it."

She took out a Rubik's Cube out of her vanity bag and gave it to Kabir. "I haven't played it for many months, but still, let's see."

He took inhaled some fresh air and flipped his fingers so fast that it became impossible to see. Within five seconds, he'd solved the Rubik's Cube. "Wow! Will you teach me?"

Kabir looked at the Cube and then at her and joked, "I can teach you, but you can't be perfect."

She asked surprisingly, "Why?"

"You must have heard the proverb 'Practice makes a man perfect'."

"Ya. I have."

Kabir giggled and said, "That's why a woman can't." They both rolled with laughter, and Kabir continued, "Okay. Okay, sorry...

CHAPTER 17

Kabir taught her slowly but surely. They both enjoyed their holidays together. The time flew with the flying of warm rays.

That day he was enjoying a TV show, cheering at his maximum, watching his favourite player. Soon, Tara came and mentioned, "Hey, Kabir."

Being disturbed midway, he ignored her and didn't even look at her and acted cheaply.

"Yes...It's a SIX! Hurrah!"

Tara was infuriated with his arrogance, so she snatched the remote from his hand and switched off the TV. "Ah! That idiot box," accused Tara.

Kabir gulped, "Hey, Tara. What's...What's the matter? I can't miss it. It's my favourite."

"I don't care. I just came here to listen to your opinion."

Kabir got puzzled. He asked, "Opinion?"

"Yup. Actually, I am going to an amusement park with Aunt. If you will come, it would be great. But, no worry, if you want to watch, you can. It's your favourite."

"Hey, it's not so…"

Soon his two small mystical advisors, Kabiroh and Kabirah, waited with their speech on his shoulders. Kabiroh said, *Hey, Kabir. She said it will be great if you would come. You must go Kabir. You can watch it later.*

Kabirah interfered saying, "Not at all, Kabir. It's a crime. Following a girl would be disrespectful for all the men in this planet. Stay foolish and enjoy TV."

They both quarrelled as usual with their voices, and Kabir, being in the middle, thought, *in what trouble I just got bogged?*

He shook his head vigorously and thought, *it was the left because of whom I was just shamed on myself, so now I will listen to Kabirah, because right is always right.*

"Hey, Kabir, are you coming with us or I should leave?"

Kabir figured out, uttering, "Ya…Ya…I mean no. I should come. No, I must come with you."

And Kabir started his drama. "I must come with you. In this despotic society who knows what will happen to anybody and…and especially to girls. There should always be a powerful, strong and a brave person to take out from any situation, like me. So, Kabirah decided. I mean, I decided to come."

Tara was completely flabbergasted by his talking. She confessed, "You know what, Kabir? Instead of Kabir, your name should be Drama King. I mean anything."

"Just go and get ready in just two minutes, I'm waiting outside. Okay?"

Tara smiled and went outside. For a while, Kabir was confused in selecting his clothes and hurried for his looks.

Outside home, Tara tapped her legs and kept an eye on her watch impatiently. She heard a voice, "There I go. Look, I'm ready."

Well, Kabir looked awesome. Tara was impressed by his appearance and gave a quick look at him. Kabir wore a white T-shirt with the wordings *Look I'm Kool*. And had ragged jeans. She coughed, clearing her throat, "Hmm…I must say, today, you are looking quite good."

Kabir's face twisted up in doubt and thought, *Quite good?*

Anyway, Kabir went with them to the amusement park. He just prayed Mrs Kanta was in good mood all through the day. As, on previous occasion, he was teased for his attitude, this time around Kabir decided to stay silent.

On entering the park, a slight breeze made the leaves crackle. The air was cool, and the beam of sunlight glowed on his skin. Soon, he realised that it's one of his favourite childhood place, where he often enjoyed playing, roaming, and riding. He was happy to be in this place with good memories. Once he entered the park, within no time he was startled by the huge crowd. Some were walking, while some were screaming being on the top of the Ferris wheel. There were many parents with their children, enjoying ice creams in one hand and balloon on the other. The hoots and howls came from the haunted house. There was a long queue at the ticket counter. And in the middle of there was a huge park with beautiful fountain. Children were cheering and chanting in cup-and-saucer ride. The whooshing of air brakes, the sizzling fries in vats of oil, pinging sound of game targets, chugging machinery, laughter, music and all that was making the place fully interesting and entertaining.

Kabir felt the bliss and became quite excited. He looked at Tara. No matter whatever happens, Mrs Kanta would never have a smile on her face. So, Kabir ignored that part and walked halfway. Mrs Kanta looked for some ice creams, and at that moment, Tara dragged Kabir and took him to a distant location.

"Now you are okay," Tara said.

Kabir was thankful for her help. Tara looked at him and Kabir stared.

"Don't look at me like that. It's really offensive."

"Oh…I'm…I'm really sorry for that."

The two strolled around the amusement park and discovered new fun-filled activity in every walkway. They were quite surprised to see people screaming aloud inside the haunted house. The whole arena was under a great evening spell. Tara bought a bag of popcorn. Kabir being a gentleman handled popcorn for her. "Thanks, Kabir."

Further they were drifting apart, enjoying every game. And in their way Tara became shocked with excitement. She looked for a roller-coaster ride. It was a huge structured pathway with a long-chained roller coaster. Tara was quite fascinated towards it. On the other hand, Kabir enjoyed the garlic taste of popcorn.

Immediately Tara demanded, "Kabir, let's go for a roller-coaster ride."

CHAPTER 18

Kabir coughed out of surprise and cleared his throat. He said, "Good joke."

"No, I'm serious," Tara muttered.

The popcorn flew in air and Kabir squeaked, "Have…Have you become mad? It's a ROLLLERR COASTERR! Just see its size, it's huge, it's dangerous, it's terrific!"

"Fools rush in where angels fear to tread."

Tara awed, "Don't act too much. It's just a rollercoaster. Just see, small children are riding with joy."

Kabir joked being afraid, "They are small that's why they don't know what fear is. Also, they haven't yet learnt the meaning of fear."

Tara was accused to see Kabir's behaviour of being scared of roller coaster. She gripped his hand and tried to take him for the ride. Kabir stuck at his place and was confused. "Tara, Tara, listen … Shh."

"Ahem, truly, I'm scared. I can't go with you. If you want, you can. I have no objection."

"Don't be foolish. I'm not going to ride alone, okay."

"Tara, please try to understand. I can't." Kabir seemed helpless and took efforts to make her understand.

She cared for him and suggested in a strong voice, "Hey, Kabir, listen. I know you can. I'm with you, okay."

Somehow, Kabir was inspired by her words and went for the ride. He shivered a bit but was confident with Tara alongside him. The roller coaster stopped near the station, and the passengers screamed, having taken their adventurous ride successfully. It was extremely thrilling and exhilarating. The sheet under his feet shook, scaring him. Kabir swallowed his fear as dreadful sweats drenched his neck.

At last the long-chained car arrived at the station, the passenger-crowd buzzing about their enthralling and horrifying experience.

"What a ride, Dad! It gave me goose bumps. It's scary!" one of the child hissed his father while passing them.

Tara clutched his hand and tried to make him seat. Suddenly, Kabir gasped, "Tara, listen. I can't, it's still terrifying. You go."

Tara dared, "Kabir, you listen, eh? Don't let the fear rule your life or else you are going to miss the most magical experiences of your life. So, now let's go."

Kabir was still not convinced but took a risk. He sat on the roller coaster and strapped the belt to his waist. For a minute, Kabir prayed for his life and remembered his parents. "Oh God, help me."

Tara sat beside Kabir. He'd thought of being together with Tara while playing badminton; however, his dream has come true rather in a creepy situation.

Finally, as the ride began slowly, both of them felt nervous and inclined their heads forward. Kabir's ears were deafened by the freaking sound of the brakes. His blood rushed through his veins as he could feel every foot he climbed.

He swallowed hard and held Tara's hand tightly and shut his eyes. The coaster slowed down as it reached its acme of the ride. Suddenly silence prevailed, and Kabir can hear his heart pounding. As he opened his eyes, the roller coaster nose-dived with high velocity, the wind slapping hard on his face, and his ears pierced with loud screams and shouts, as he experienced an adrenaline rush. With every twist and turn, he could feel his body tremble. Kabir's heart was on his mouth, and he felt a sudden heaviness. After a 15-minute-long horrifying ride, the car reached the station. But still Kabir felt the movement of his body. His fear had gone out of his disillusioned mind. He unbuckled the seat belt and stepped outside hurriedly. He was exhausted. So, he inhaled and exhaled. Tara came, patted his shoulder and asked him, "So, Kabir, how was the ride?"

Kabir's legs trembled, and he looked at Tara and grumbled, "Was it a ride? It's called a shortcut path to hell. It just nailed me."

Tara bent out of shape and urged, "You are such a coward. I hate cowards."

It made Kabir to think. He hissed, "I'm brave," in a low tone, so Tara implied, "What?"

Kabir's mouth twitched, "I...I...I mean I really liked that ride. I was just joking. Seriously, it was adventurous. And you know what? I like adventures. I would tell my mom to bring me here every day for the ride."

Tara joked, "You really liked it. Good. Let's have one more ride, please."

Kabir yelled, "NOO! I mean, it has been very late and ya, your aunt."

Tara focussed on her aunt and Kabir took a breather. "Oh God, I would never have a ride again. Never," he judged.

INTERVIEW

"Ah! Man. You know what? All girls love horrifying stuffs. Don't you?"

The interviewer smiled and gasped, "Ya."

"Good. But why they include others to join them. I mean if you want to ride, then go, what is stopping you?"

He gasped, "But NO! They always need someone. Why can't they be independent?"

The interviewer said with a smile, "Maybe, they want someone to pay off their bills. And perhaps she wanted to make you know what the meaning of thrill is, action and adventure."

Kabir felt disgusted and curled his hands under his arms. She pleaded, "Okay, okay, I'm sorry. Please continue. What happened next?"

Kabir looked at her and took another sip. After five seconds, he continued...

CHAPTER 19

Kabir dared not to see Tara as he experienced one of his most piercing moments ever. Thinking about that ride gave him the jitters.

Since he had summer holidays, every day was like a Sunday. It was quite radiant and luminous. Kabir reached home after a healthy jog, sweating like a pig. He then drank a glass of chilled water and relaxed under the coolness of the fan.

He made it to the bathroom to get freshen up when he heard muffled voices from Tara's room upstairs. He slowly went upstairs to get a closer look. He looked from the edge of the door and observed that Tara was talking to someone. Kabir heard silently and slipped inside her room.

"Oh! Hi, Kabir."

Kabir looked vaguely around the room and wished, "Ya. Hi, Tara. Who's she?"

Tara introduced her, "Oops, sorry, I just forgot to tell you."

Tara hugged her tightly and muttered, "She is my bestest of the bestest friend!"

Kabir said, "Oh, I see!"

He greeted him with a handshake. "Myself, Kabir."

"Gauri, thanks."

It was a warm handshake. She had hair with thick natural curls, was fair-skinned and looked pretty. Both Tara and Gauri can easily be fooled to be taken as sisters on any given day. But felt like she was on pins and needles. Kabir could gauge her mood.

Tara squeaked, "Gauri, you don't worry, okay. Everything will be fine."

Kabir felt confused and distracted and asked, "Hey, Tara. What's the matter?"

Tara yelled, "Nothing much, Kabir." And Tara and Gauri soon started discussing on a matter. Kabir, being stunned, told, "Ahem. Tara, I think I can help you if you want. But first let me know what the matter is."

Tara took a breath and grieved, "Kabir, Gauri is from a big family. And his father is a businessman and loves to buy antiques."

"Aha," Kabir gasped.

"And today, when Gauri was playing with her flying disk, the disk flew through the window and broke the glass painting piece. When Gauri entered the house, she saw the broken pieces of glass painting shattered on the floors. It's the painting her father needs for tomorrow's assignment. It's urgent. That's why we are worried. If her father comes to know about it, then…she will be grounded."

Kabir expressed his concern and said, "Oops!"

"Hey, Gauri, idea. Why don't you just buy it from online websites or from an artwork shop? You can easily get that same painting."

Tara smiled on his innocence. She mentioned, "Kabir, it's only one of a kind. It's the famous painting *Ada* by Tim Steyer."

Kabir was shocked, as he knew the true value of Tim's masterpiece. "Oh man!"

Seeing Kabir's reactions, Gauri was upset, and realised that she had done a huge mistake, and would be punished. She was down in the dumps as her eyes bore tears.

Tara assisted her in to her room and said, "Hey, Gauri, don't worry. We will find a way out. Okay, so don't cry."

Kabir thought about the problem, with both Kabirah and Kabiroh in tow. Kabirah advised, *Kabir, just think. She needs help. Just think out of the box.* And instantly, Kabir got a brilliant idea.

He uttered, "Tara, Gauri. Don't worry, I can make it."

"What! What!" Their voices echoed simultaneously with surprise.

Tara boggled and coughed, "Kabir … It's serious."

Kabir said confidently, "Me too."

Tara said precisely, "Kabir, you don't even know the P of Painting. How can you think of making such a masterpiece?"

Kabir grinned and suggested, "For your kind information, miss, I'm Kabir Malhotra."

Tara said with confusion, "So what?"

Kabir squeaked, "Miss, I have been the best painter in whole of the state. I have also been selected for nationals, and that too twice."

Kabir blew his own trumpet, and Tara looked at him surprisingly, and Gauri's face, drowned in sorrow, lifted with hope.

Tara was surprised to know he had such a hidden talent. She couldn't believe her ears, but she had to keep trust on him as a friend.

Gauri stated with a request, "Kabir, please. If you can help me out of this, then I would be thankful to you. Please."

Kabir assured, "Sure, Gauri. I will."

Gauri controlled her emotions. Kabir rose and grunted, "Tara, I need your help to figure out this. It's a challenge for me, but I would love to do this."

"Come on, let's go and check the actual painting there." Gauri, Tara and Kabir went to investigate the spot. The three teens soon reached Gauri's house, and Tara and Kabir were surprised.

It was a huge mansion with a10-car garage with white-uniformed drivers in tow. There was a big garden in front of the house with variety of trees and a fountain in the middle. Ferns and mosses covered the sideways of the house. In the cold, sunny morning, Tara, Gauri and Kabir stepped into the house.

When they entered the hall, an old man in a black suit greeted them respectfully.

"My name is Charles," his voice trembled though he spoke tight.

"He is our house keeper, but more like a family. He has been serving us for 10 years." Kabir and Tara wished him, and they went and checked the site where the incident, rather accident, happened.

Kabir was shocked to see the painting's condition: shards of broken glasses spread around the room. He tilted his head upward and saw the place where it was hung earlier. He noticed everything and said, "Gauri, I need a day. You just call us before your father arrives. It will be better if you would come to inform us in the morning."

Gauri stated, "Yup, sure."

Gauri insisted them to have a cup of coffee. And Tara had no other choice but to say yes. But Tara was fighting with her fate as Charles made a mistake, and the coffee poured on her dress. (God! It was a cold coffee.)

"I will change it." Tara was disgusted.

"Okay. Tara, let's go, we need some paints and brushes. And, Gauri, don't worry, okay. Chill out."

Soon both left to shop for painting-related stuffs. Kabir searched for those colours and found it.

Once they finished the shopping, Kabir browsed the web to collect data—images and dimensions of the canvas—regarding *Ada*. So, finally, Kabir was all set to begin his painting work. With all the experience she'd gained from his national-level painting competition, he stroked the brush with a deft touch across the canvas. The strokes of every hair of brush made a kind of illusion.

Evening turned to night as Kabir gave his best shot, still not complete with his work. Tara came and said in a low tone, "Kabir, you should eat now. It's ten on the clock and…and you haven't eaten anything during the evening."

Kabir wet his lips and said, "Tara, you go. I will eat later."

Tara was miffed at him and hissed, "Nope. If you are not going to eat. Then, me too." Even when she was angry, she looked elegant.

Kabir saw her and paid attention to her, "Eh? Tara, don't be silly." But Tara remained glum.

Finally, Kabir decided to eat. "Okay, miss, you won." She reciprocated with a beautiful smile, with her face brightening. The two sat on the dining table and had a late dinner.

Kabir almost completed his painting a she enjoyed the art of colouring. On the other hand, Tara too assisted him and gave full support until the task was completed. Night turned into early morning, as they gave final touches to the painting. No one felt sleepy anymore, especially Tara. At last, after five hours, Kabir took a breather and yawned, "I did it, Tara. And now…," and he dozed off on her lap, murmuring something.

Tara whispered, "Kabir, are you all right?" Kabir, being tired, slept like a baby. Tara smiled at him and smirked, "Kabir, you!" She looked at him and waved his hair. She was completely smitten and her heart throbbed, a feeling of a heart merging with another. She felt nostalgic and felt wetness inside her. She couldn't help herself out.

After a minute of dilemma and fighting her inner demons, she laid him on the bed, covered him with a bed cover and wished him "Sweet dreams, Kabir."

After a short nap, Kabir was disturbed by the sunlight streaming through the windows. He looked at his wall clock, which was showing seven, and he felt relaxed. His eyes were tired with dark circles. But somehow, he managed to wake up.

He went upstairs and saw Gauri and Tara watching his painting. Kabir scratched his head and stood silent to know their reviews.

Tara saw him and said mockingly, "Kabir, what is this?"

He turned nervous and felt criticised. The angry look on Tara soon transformed into a widening smile. She praised, "Kabir, don't panic. It's awesome. You just whacked me. No one can do better than you."

It was a breath-taking painting piece; by comparing both the pictures, Tim himself wouldn't be able to identify which is original. Gauri came closer to him and thanked him. She didn't know to express her inner happiness. She just smiled and thanked Kabir and Tara, 12 times (may be less).

She informed, "Tara, Kabir, it's going to be late. Dad would be coming home. I must reach home as soon as possible. And, Kabir, thanks would be very little for the job you did."

Kabir welcomed her and helped her carry the canvas. "Gauri, it's quite heavy. You can't make it alone. I think you wouldn't mind if we help you the way out, to your house."

"Wow! How you got that?" Charles asked.

"It's all over Kabir's fingers," joked Tara. And Charles returned to the kitchen.

Kabir and Tara wished her luck and were leaving the mansion when they found a man with gelled blonde hair and branded black suit standing.

"Dad!"

Tara looked surprised as they haven't still hung the painting on the wall.

"Gauri, what's that?" he pointed to the precious piece of painting lying on the floor.

Gauri stammered hearing her father's terror-filled voice. "Dad. Act...Actually."

"And who are they?" his voice was rough and broken.

"My name is Kabir and..."

"Did I ask you?" he squeaked.

Kabir and Tara were stunned by his attitude, enraged upon his grumbling voice. For a minute, there was a deadly silence in the room.

Then he yelled at his daughter, "I asked you something, Gauri!"

"Dad, yesterday I was..." And she narrated the entire story in short. Kabir and Tara, being still there, were searching for a reason to leave. "Sir, if you don't mind, can we go?" Tara pleaded.

"No one will go. First, Gauri. Without my permission—I mean, how? You can't be forgiven." As a father, he said what everyone else's would do.

"But..."

Everybody looked at Kabir, as he spoke, "Sir, story isn't completed."

"Sorry. I couldn't get you." Her father looked confused.

Kabir breathed and said, "Sir. You can't blame your daughter. She is not guilty. Yesterday, when I came to see it, the broken pieces of glasses were lying on that shag carpet."

"First, when I saw the nail hanged above, it was too high. And the window was placed at a low height. So, the disk couldn't have reached such a height. Second, the glass used in Tim's masterpiece is made up of palladium-based silica glass, which can't be broken too easily by such a disk. Third, I found a small scratch over your orange wall right above the drawer, which is made by that disk. So, from my assumption Gauri is not guilty. Okay."

"Then who did it?" her father was roused to anxiety.

"He is Charles!" Kabir pointed.

Charles, staring and sweating profusely, urged, "How can I do?"

"It is too sure that Gauri was out when it happened. And you were in. When I came yesterday, I saw you busy with your fingers. A butler being there with the house for 10 years, how can he make a mistake while serving tea? Unless he had been glued."

"Second, I saw you with gloves and a broom resting at the side of the wall. You might be cleaning the room and while using the broom, you might have hit the painting and thus it went wrong."

"Third, most importantly, I saw fear and sweat in your face. Is there anything so serious for a butler unless he had done anything wrong? What else anyone wants from a culprit?"

Charles went down on his knee and gasped, "Sorry, sir. It was my fault. While cleaning, it just slipped and hit the floor. I'm really sorry, sir."

"Hey, it's okay, Charles, you accepted, that's all." For the first time, Kabir saw such a level of hypocrisy by an adult.

After a short interval, her father looked at the painting and gasped, "Huh! It can be passable."

And turning towards Kabir, with utmost credibility, her father thanked him, and he showed up.

While talking to Charles again, Gauri took them to the garden square.

"I don't know how to thank you, but…" And she hugged Kabir. Kabir felt shy and blushed.

"Cool," Tara accused.

Gauri waved goodbye and thanked both for their support.

Kabir and Tara were on their way back home. Tara felt a bit jealous when Gauri hugged Kabir. Maybe, it's a kind of friendship she wanted from him.

Both walked across the road and as twilight fell. Tara grumbled, "Kabir, you did a great job. I'm impressed."

Kabir listened to her statement and became dreamy. He doubted her faith as if it's true or not.

She commented, "You are good, hon. I like you."

Kabir stretched his eyebrows in surprise. He never thought that Tara would like him. The line "I like you" revolved around his mind steadily and he jumped up high, cheering, "Yippee!"

Tara saw him, as he got too much excited, and said, "Kabir, are you all right?"

Kabir coughed, "Ya…Ya…Sure." Looking at the roadside concrete structures, he asked, "So, you like me? I mean you like me?"

"No, I don't like you. I mean I don't like you. Does it change the emotion or are you going to teach grammar instead?"

Kabir was on cloud ten, instead of nine, and became quite happy. He shouted, looking at the sky, "This feeling is beautiful."

Tara smiled seeing his innocence and said, "Kabir, let's go home."

CHAPTER 20

Aww! So cute. Tara searched through Kabir's bag secretly and found some of his childhood photos. *Cool, he is dancing wearing a skirt*. When children are small, they are made to wear attires of opposite sexes. (Don't know why.)

She found some crushed papers with written words. She read some of his roughs and got irritated. *I think he would have been trying very hard to write something special. May be a story, who knows?*

Then she found everyday stuffs like shampoo, deodorants, his Walkman, earphones, and more.

She then found a well-folded piece of paper in his satchel. She opened the paper and read it. It was a letter from Uncle Iyer. She became morose and agitated after reading such an intimate and profound writing. And she was surprised to know about it and rushed to see Kabir.

On the other hand, Kabir jogged around the park.

The park was fresh and green. Kabir sat on a wooden bench, exhausted. A small girl who wore her hair in plaits with disgusted look dashed beside Kabir.

"You know what my teacher said to me?" she acclaimed. Kabir nodded.

"She told me that my cells are poor enough, that's why I always get sick." Kabir nodded surprisingly.

"But how these cells form? Why aren't they good in me?" she said.

Kabir raised his eyebrows and stated, "Ah! I must tell you that I'm best in false biology. But I do know how cells are formed. These cells are formed from pre-existing cells. They divide and form daughter cells and these cells again divide and form more daughter cells and it continues. I know it's difficult to understand."

She became thoughtful and gasped, "Why cells don't form son cells?"

Kabir blamed himself. He was shocked and joked, "Maybe cells are." Kabir was wordless.

"Hey, leave it. But I must tell you that you are strong, your teacher must be blamed. She must be punished for such language and humiliation. She must be imprisoned. What you say?"

"You can't say like that about my mom," and fled the scene within a second. Kabir looked at the sky with moving clouds and gasped.

Suddenly, he saw Tara approaching him. He was surprised and grumbled, "Hey, good morning, Tara. Want to join me?"

She took a breather and said, "You cheater. You like Meera Sharma, you are a good reader, wants to write a novel only to meet her and many more. You didn't tell me anything about your dreams. Why, Kabir?"

Kabir was completely stumped and said, "Act... Actually. Leave it, Tara." And he turned back with a sigh.

Tara felt depressed. She encountered, gripping his shoulder back, "Hey, Kabir. What actually? You know what? You are a coward who don't follow your dreams."

Kabir couldn't control his senses and squeaked, "Tara, that's all! What you know about me? Tara, listen, I don't want to revive those memories. I lost my partner only because of those stupid books and my reckless dreams. That's why I vanquished my desires." Kabir kept his chin up only to show others that he was fine and good. But deep inside, he was still struggling to cope up with that incident.

Kabir relaxed his breath and said in a suggestive way, "Sometimes we get busy in chasing our dreams that we forget about the dear ones who had paved the true path for our dream."

Tara was not deterred by his words, but she just wanted him to be right on his path of dreams. "Kabir, I can understand your feelings. But what happened is not the matter, but what will happen surely defines your future." "And that 'will happen' belongs to what you decide to do."

Kabir was silent for a second and squeaked, "No, Tara. It's not so easy," and he fled the scene.

"Listen, Ka..." And he disappeared. Tara couldn't understand his problem.

Kabir reached home, exhausted. He was bathed in sweats and felt depressed by her question. He looked up and thought about his partner.

After some time, Tara came to home and looked for Kabir. She went to his room and saw him in a deep sleep. Tara, concerned about Kabir, let him sleep.

After the park incident, for many days, Kabir didn't talk to Tara. He was just ignoring her. Maybe he didn't want her to be a part of his life. But on the other hand, Tara felt quite ignored and annoyed, and those ignoring days lengthened.

INTERVIEW

"In my opinion, I is inversely proportional to F, where I is the ignorance and F is the friendship between them."

"I was surely ignoring her but had of deep, pent-up emotion towards her."

The interviewer looked at him and asked, "Then what happened? Did she talk to you or did you?"

Kabir smirked and said, "She was more than a friend. She made it, and I had my ego. But she…"

CHAPTER 21

Kabir woke up and saw that it was lunchtime! He was shocked and realised that he had slept the whole morning.

When he stood up, he was perplexed to see books all around him: some on his bedside, some near his table and some on the floor. Kabir was irritated by Tara's prank and called her.

Finally, Kabir jumped out of his bed and watched out for Tara, who was having her lunch, and provoked her, "Tara, what are you doing? It's awful!"

Tara didn't pay attention to him and was busy with her eating. It infuriated Kabir, so he grabbed her shoulder and dragged her out of the chair to his room. Pointing towards the books, Kabir claimed, "Tara, what is this?"

Tara, being kind enough, said tenderly, "Kabir, it's your choices."

Kabir was uncertain by her words and asked, "What do you mean?"

"Look. The books are there on the bed, on the table, on the floor." Kabir couldn't make out what she told, still being doubtful.

Tara smiled and said, "Kabir, the books on the bed tells you how much you were hypnotised by its attraction that you lost your partner. You read those books day and night. That's why they are on the bed."

"The books on the floor states you what you did when you lost your partner. You just threw them on the floor."

"But, Kabir, in between these two odds, there lies the secret of your destiny. Look, the books lying on your table. It can help you to be consistent with your dreams. Who knows, the books on the table may be yours, one day. But for that one day, Kabir, please try. Please, Kabir, for me."

Kabir became desperate on hearing her words.

"Kabir, we all have dreams, we all have desires, but what we do is what we choose. And you choose to write, you can't deny your destiny."

Her words really melted his heart. At that moment, he felt like he was on the edge of the cliff with Tara's confidence on the bright side and his cruel past on the dark side.

Being once again in dilemma, he met his intuitive friends. On his left, he heard Kabiroh claiming, *Hey, Kabir, don't listen to her. Girls are gamblers. She will ruin you.*

On the right, he heard Kabirah advising, *don't listen to that Kabiroh gangster.*

Kabir, she is your friend, may be more than a friend. And she is fighting for your dreams. It's good. You must join her.

From his left-side brain he heard his inner voice chuckling, *Ha-ha...Ho-ho...Kabir, just remember what she did when you went for the badminton, and of course that roller-coaster ride. How can you forget those?* Kabir was provoked by those suggestions and can't think straight.

Tara saw him fighting with his inner demons and neared him and grabbed his hands and said, "Kabir, please." Her hand was soft and warm. Kabir blushed and became hesitant. He saw her eyes, which was full of aspirations and faith. He couldn't decide what to do and gave a funny look to show his awkwardness.

It became too much, he thought.

Suddenly Kabirah voiced, *Lucky boy! Kabir, always remember, no one is going to fight for your dreams and it's a second chance you are getting. I don't think anyone would ever leave this chance.*

Kabir cleared his throat and quivered, "Hey... hey, Tara. It's okay. I will read...and write."

Tara questioned, "Promise?"

He nodded. "Ya...Ya...I promise."

She left his hands and became happy. "That's good."

She was leaving the room when Kabir interrupted, "Tara?"

She looked back and nodded. "Don't you have any dreams or, in my language, any desire?"

She bit her lips and thought for a second and replied, "Hmm...Yup, I have one. I want to perform in India's biggest dance festival, which is going to held this year in Chandigarh. I have been practising for many months."

She breathed lungful and continued, "I want to be a dancer."

Kabir became a bit nostalgic to listen to her desire, as he never knew that Tara was a dancer, nor he ever asked her about it. He was confused but cleared off his doubt as he said, "Okay, Tara. You help me to write my novel and I will help you in dancing. Promise?"

She giggled and gave a perfect smile, stating, "But how? You stupid, you don't know a bit of dance."

"I think my presence will be enough."

Tara smiled and said, "Sure. But promise me, okay. No, cheating."

Kabir accepted her demand with a grin as she left the room.

Kabir scratched his head and smiled. *She is definitely going to make me a writer,* he thought and laughed.

123

CHAPTER 22

Kabir started his practice and borrowed books from Tara's shelves. He started feeling lucky and joyous not only outward but also inward. He made fun of Tara, and both entertained the whole house, but Mrs Kanta was troubled by their playful activities.

Kabir looked for vocabulary and writing tips and busied himself by surfing the web for different kinds of tips and quotes. He was excited and became good at web surfing. Nearby, he also joined the English class.

That day Kabir was reading a new novel with full concentration, *The Lost Baby* by Jeffer Lever. He did his best to grasp the essence of the novel. That time Tara called her, "Hey, Kabir. Let's go. We are going for a walk."

Kabir looked at her and smiled. "Sure, wait a minute." He bookmarked the page by folding its edge and left the book on his table. Tara was glad to see the change in Kabir's attitude. She gave an affectionate smile. Kabir gasped, "What! Let's go."

Tara ran out with a smiling face and joked, "It's just a prank. Go and read."

Kabir beamed with smile and said, "Tara, you." He chased her; she ran to her room to protect herself from Kabir. Kabir was in no mood to leave as he followed her upstairs and entered her room. He grabbed a pillow and hit Tara softly. "Hey, Kabir. Stop."

Kabir hither five times and said, "No…" Tara wanted to say something, but instead she stiffened her arm and shouted, "Stoppp."

Kabir stood still, hearing her shout. For a second, the entire house was silent. Tara slipped her hand, grabbed another pillow and hit Kabir. Kabir grumbled, "Heyy…Tara. It's not fair."

Now both were in action mode, converting the room into a war zone. Soon the room was clouded with the foam stuffing from the pillows, which flew and left the mark all through the room like a trail of wakes behind the boat.

"Hey, Tara, it's not fair."

"Sorry, mister, everything is fair in love and war." She gave him another good hit with her pillow.

Kabir made shield out of his pillow to protect himself from her chapati shots. He questioned her, "Then what is here going on? Love or war, eh?"

Tara, being busy in attacking, without much thought, mumbled, "Maybe love."

Kabir felt happy and grumbled, "Me too."

She stopped hitting and asked, "What! When a girl says 'What', it's not because she didn't hear you. She just warns you to take your words back, buddy. That's psychology."

He simpered, "Just kidding."

She looked down, perhaps disappointingly. And in that fraction of a second, Kabir took a chance and whacked the pillow on her right shoulder. Since Tara was not expecting a hit, she fell to the floor as her foot twisted and hit the tiles and her head hit the bedpost and was knocked unconscious.

Kabir became agitated as his eyelids drooped and his heart began to palpitate. He rushed and knelt down and held her head. He observed blood spurting out of her head, covering whole of her left face. Kabir's hand had reddened, and he got nervous. He cried, "Aunttt! Aunt! Hurry up."

Mrs Kanta—who was making tea—on hearing the loud voice—dashed to Tara's room; she was shocked to see Tara in such a condition. She held her head, and instructed Kabir to call a doctor, immediately.

Kabir was shell-shocked and was hit with a panic attack. He didn't hear what Mrs Kanta said. For a second, his mind went blank. Then he came to his senses and saw Mrs Kanta trying to wake Tara up. Kabir ran downstairs, searched for the telephone directory and found the doctor's number. He called one of the doctors from the available numbers and waited with bated breath.

After a 15-minute wait, the doctor arrived and Kabir took him upstairs to Tara's room. The doctor insisted them to wait outside. It was heart-breaking for Kabir. He kept his fingers crossed and did a heart-felt prayer for speedy recovery. For the first time, Kabir saw Aunt crying, an impossible happening to witness in his lifetime. Since it was a critical situation, he went near her and consoled her, saying, "Tara will be fine, Aunt, believe me."

It was no better statement at that moment to give anyone support. After half hour, the door opened. Kabir stood with a jolt. Seeing Kabir's troublesome face, the doctor said without any suspense, "She is still unconscious, but out of danger, so don't worry. It would have been more serious if I had been a second late."

Kabir took a breather after listening to the doctor's statement. The doctor smiled looking at him and said, "These are some medicines. Okay." Kabir took the medicines and thanked him.

It was heartening to hear doctor's positive response. He summoned up courage and went inside the room. Although he had visited her room many a times, he felt different this time around and had a weird feeling. Soon he fixed his eyes on the bed.

Tara lay on her bed with a bandage wrapped around her forehead.

Kabir felt very bad to see her in such a state. He went near her and sat beside her at the edge of the bed. The room was warm, and the sunlight pored through the window and fell on Tara's face. Kabir observed her serene face for a minute, being attracted, and felt an aura behind her. Kabir bent and shook his hand over her face. He smoothed the hair to one side that was falling on her face. Kabir sighed and bent and kissed her forehead softly.

He looked at her, her eyes still fixed at its place. He then held her right hand, which was warm, and said, "You know, Tara. I was having a partner, a friend. With him, life was interesting yet dull. He was always with me. But I never understood his presence. He went and you came in my life. And… Now I don't want to lose you."

He was choked with emotion and was busy controlling his tears. He gulped, "You came and changed me. You gave me a new hope, a new desire, a new friend. My dreams were scattered like clouds, but you shaped them all. Tara, you… you will always be my bestest friend."

The sun was at its peak.

It was around two o'clock, and Kabir stayed in her room, half-sleeping. The afternoon went with a deadly silence. Suddenly, he felt some movement from Tara's left hand. He woke up with wet eyes and got excited to see Tara batting her eyelashes. She then slowly opened her eyes, out of tiredness and medication. Kabir responded by returning a big, wide smile.

"I'm really sorry, Tara."

She looked tired but signalled Kabir with her eye to come closer. He approached near her to hear what she was mouthing. She gasped out very lightly, "You are a really bad actor."

Kabir smiled and once again became lively, laughing without a pause. She countered with a smirk. The time stood still as the room was filled with laughter.

"Take rest, Tara. Okay?" Kabir said, covering her with a blanket, and left the room.

He was in a bittersweet mood, so he walked to joggers' park after a nap and sat on the wooden bench. He had disturbing thoughts of morning happiness involving Tara; he tried hard to flush those thoughts from his mind when his two inner soulmates popped on his two shoulders Kabir was irritated to see them. He said, *Not now, buddies. I'm not okay*.

Kabirah said, *you are not okay. Hmmm…It happens to everybody when he or she is in love with someone.* He lured him.

Hey, there's nothing. Okay, we are just, just good friends, Kabir explained.

Kabiroh mocked, *Yup, they are just friends, you know, Kabirah.*

Kabirah chided, *Okay, so would you kiss her forehead and grab her hands and would tell her everything only in the name of just friends?*

Kabir looked thoughtful for a moment. He wanted to tell her what he felt, but he can't. He was such a coward. Due to fatigue and headache, he screamed at them and both disappeared in a flash. Kabir snickered as if he knew the answer for their question.

CHAPTER 23

With every passing day, Tara's showed improvement in her road to recovery, and she very well knew that Kabir would be by her side always. And Kabir exactly did what he was supposed to. He came and monitored her routinely whether she had her medicines on time. There was some inner bonding happening between the two, which both recognised yet acted as if unknown to them.

Within a week, Tara was back to her usual being, fit and fine. On few occasions, she had headaches, but Kabir saw to her that she was okay and well medicated. One day, Kabir took her to joggers' park for a fresh morning walk. It was a bright day with clean blue sky. They sat on the long dew-filled wooden bench as Tara started the conversation by thanking him. "Thanks, Kabir, for doing so much. I'm really thankful."

Kabir scratched his head and smiled. "No, Tara, it's okay. I...I'm your friend. And a friend will always be there for her, whenever, whatever, wherever she would be." She blushed and smiled.

It was quite odd as both were shy for the first time to continue with their chat.

After a minute of silence, Tara coughed, "Kabir, let's go for a picnic this Sunday. My friends are going to Waki Woods. So, it will be great if you could join us. So, Will you?"

Kabir shook his head and thought for a second. After clearing his throat, he replied, "Hmm…Tara, I could but—"

She interrupted and pleaded, "Don't say no, na. Please. For me."

All girls are expert in luring. No one can outdo them. If we leave them to terrorist, they would win their heart by their art of luring. It's all in their genes, Kabir thought.

But he wanted to say an emphatic "no" because…because. But he didn't have any concrete reason. He just thought to simply reply in negative.

He uttered something but was cross-answered by Tara. At last he had no other choice but to accept her invite. Kabir gave a perfect smile and nodded. They talked for over an hour, giggling and laughing, as they realised they enjoyed each other's company.

***

It was four days before the expedition. Kabir tried his best to keep those days cherished in his memory for lifelong. Meanwhile, he followed his desire and attended English classes, which kept him busy with no time to see or talk to Tara.

But Tara longed to talk to him, after so much days of no communication whatsoever. Although it was only three days, for Tara it felt like three months. (Theory of relativity?)

She asked her aunt, "Aunt, where is Kabir?"

Mrs Kanta, who was busy in the kitchen, answered, "Oh! I saw him in his room. He was busy with pen and papers."

She nodded and went to his room. She peeped through the edge of the door and saw Kabir thoughtful, sitting in his chair. He was busy with pen and papers, made paper balls as he crushed it in the dustbin every few minutes, in disappointment. He was irritated—Ah! —and scratched his head. Tara bit her lips and looked upset. She backed to her room and thought of helping him to find a good story, but to no avail. As a final choice, she prayed, "Please God, help Kabir get a good plot."

It was Sunday, and they were ready with their backpacks for their picnic to Waki Woods. Even Mrs Kanta joined the picnic all dressed up after so much cajoling from Tara's friend's mom, which Kabir disliked. So, the whole house was ready for the trip. Gauri too had joined the trip. She was excited to see Kabir; she came closer and gave him a big hug. Tara disapproved Gauri's behaviour and gave her the cold shoulder.

They booked a private bus and reached Waki Woods by evening. They enjoyed the picturesque sunset on the bank of a lovely river. They then set camps for the night. Soon, as the evening darkened, a pearl white moon shone on the sky on the backdrop of a lovely river. Later, they gathered around a campfire and exhibited their talents— played games, sang songs, danced a lot, and many more. Kabir focussed on Tara's smile and enjoyed her presence every moment, with no care shown on 20-odd unknown person gathered around. Tara was his true friend and beyond. Malvika, one of Tara' friend, played guitar and invited Tara to join her. Kabir saw Tara shying away. He thought it's human nature to act shy in front of a crowd, in which everybody's focus is on you with great expectation. They all requested and begged her to sing. And Kabir finally voiced, "Tara, please." She smirked and readied herself by clearing her voice. She sat near Malvika and listened to her tunes. Kabir was excited to listen to Tara's song, for the very first time.

All clapped and cheered along. Malvika hit the first chord of the string, producing a deep, long sound that echoed throughout the woods. And soon Tara's sweet voice took over and mesmerised the audience gathered around. Kabir was awestruck to see her talent and clapped and encouraged her all through her singing; he felt like a happiest person in the world. She saw Kabir and gave him her ever-beautiful smile as a return gift.

After so much of entertainment, all had their sumptuous and delicious dinner. Soon, Kabir realised that it was more than a picnic, or so-called trekking trip. As midnight neared and new day dawned, the entire camp went silent and returned to take rest.

Suddenly, Tara heard some unusual sounds, so she woke, alerted herself and gathered strength and came outside of her tent. She heard the sound of paper crushing and saw Kabir, sitting alone and crying over his crushed papers, "Ah! God. Help me out."

Tara smiled and sat close beside him, their shoulders touching, which Kabir failed to notice. He said surprisingly, "Oh! Tara, hi," and hid the crushed papers between his legs.

Tara replied, "Ya, hi. So…What are you doing with those hidden papers?"

Kabir bowed with a sigh and said, "Nothing much." He put those crushed papers behind his back.

"Oh! I see. You are hiding something from me."

"Na, nothing."

Tara sighed and pointed out, "Kabir, don't hide. I know you are trying your best to write a story, but there's nothing to hide, at least from me."

Kabir awed and grumbled, "Tara, there's everything to hide. I can't even write a sentence. No plot, no story, no characters, nothing. Fully blank," he frowned dejectedly.

Tara bit her lip and stated, "Hey, Kabir. That's not your fault. You are trying your best, and that's great."

Kabir was still silent and disappointed. Tara became worried about him and said, "Ka...Kab... Kabir, listen. Just observe around, and there are endless ideas. Connect with nature, she will give you the answers to every impossibility."

Kabir was upset for three things: first, he was not able to write a story; second, he doubted his belief and desire to become a writer an impossibility; and third, Tara was trying her best to motivate him.

Kabir felt bad and was looked down with disappointment.

Tara looked worried seeing Kabir in such a state, so she held his hands and said, "Kabir, don't worry."

At that very moment, he wanted to pour out everything what he felt. Still looking at the ground, he said, "You know what, Tara? When I went to Pune to meet Meera Sharma, I expected too much, or you can say I believed too much. I waited for three hours inside a bookstore. And she didn't come. I was hopeless. For a minute, I was lost. But suddenly, where the hell, and I struck an idea and started writing a novel. I got busy in it so much so that I didn't notice that I was losing my near and dear ones. When I looked back, it was too late. And now I'm unable to write a single sentence."

Tara could easily feel his pain and was concerned about Kabir's well-being. She took a breather and started narrating her story. "Kabir, when I was of four, I lost my mom. But my father and my brother never made me feel her absence. I was quite happy with them, especially my father. He always made me laugh, made me feel good and said me one thing, 'Tara, inside you just light up that fire, because you are the one who can inspire.' He was my hero, my everything. And of course, my big bro. We would always have a pillow fight before our sleep. Everything was going good until that Friday ruined my life. It was a Friday evening. We were all very happy that day because I had won first prize in a dance competition," she giggled.

"And...And...with that joy-filled heart we went to a restaurant that night. My brother was driving the car with my father beside. We were talking and enjoying the moment. I turned up the radio to listen to one of my favourite songs. I was just listening to the music when all of a sudden, a moving truck stopped before us. My brother hit the brakes with full force, but the car screeched and slammed right into the back of that truck. I still remember that moment of my life. The windshield shattered into pieces. My brother's head hit the steering wheel and...and my father..."

She swallowed and continued, "That three seconds destroyed my entire life. I was half unconscious. I could easily sense the amount of blood flowing through my head. My brother and father were taken in stretchers. The last picture I could remember was the ICU's light hanging right upon me as my eyes blurred and became blank."

She again swallowed and said in a low voice, "I...I lost my father and...and my brother. It took me three years to recover from that terrible incident. Now, I'm living with my grandparents in Chandigarh."

For the first time, on listening to her story, Kabir realised the pain she was carrying all through her life. Tara nodded and said, clearing her eyes, "Kabir, time is so cruel, na. It takes our dear ones and gives us the hardest part of life to live, although it teaches us how to live, but it fails to teach us how to forget those memories."

"But you know what? I do really want to show my father that I am one of the greatest dancer. And I will really meet him when I win the show."

"Show?"

"Haven't I told you about India's biggest dance festival?"

Kabir nodded.

Tara shifted her neck and bent over Kabir's shoulder and gasped, "I will show him."

Kabir felt uncomfortable and said, patting her shoulder, "It's okay, Tara." He felt uneasy when she came closer to him and grabbed his T-shirt tightly. Kabir became nervous and gasped, "If you would continue to hold me like this, I…I…I would be more nervous."

Tara realised how close she sat near Kabir and freaked; clearing her eyes, she said, "Oh! I'm sorry." Kabir grinned foolishly. But suddenly his eyes lit up and his face brightened. He soon realised that he already had a story. An idea sparked him. He became active and squeaked standing on the trunk of the broken tree. He was so excited that Tara was confused to see him. He held her two shoulders and said with excitement, "Tara, Tara, Tara. You are great. Thank you so much."

Tara was still confused to see such a funny behaviour from Kabir and said, "What do you mean, Kabir?"

Kabir confessed, "Tara, I got a story. I got a story."

His eyes glittered with amusement and broke his boredom by stretching his hands and added,

"A teen who wants to be a writer only to meet his favourite writer. It means I'm going to write a story on myself."

Tara gave her trademark smile as she stood and said, "Kabir, it's a brilliant idea! You can write about yourself—your feelings, your experiences, your stories."

Kabir was on cloud nine (no cloud ten). He said, "My story would be a fiction, of course, but it would be inspired by true events of my life."

"Yes, and there will be every bit of your life you experienced, from waiting for your partner to me."

Kabir excitedly said, dancing under the sky, "Yes, it will be fantastic. Publishers need that."

"But wait, what will be the title?" Tara questioned.

Kabir thought, biting his finger nails, and said, "The title will be *I Want to Be a Writer*."

Tara became so happy to see Kabir. She stood on the trunk and lifted the pen and acted, "So, here I want to present India's youngest bestsellerrr... Kabir Malhotra!"

Kabir and Tara laughed loudly that Gauri and Malvika came out of their respective tent stirred with their blurry eyes and quarrelled, "Hey, both of you. What the hell are you doing in the middle of the night? Can't you keep quiet and let us sleep?" They went inside their tent after scolding them.

Tara and Kabir controlled their laughter for a minute, but soon they were rolling in grass, unable to control their laughter. They enjoyed their lone moment and talked about the plot and the characters of the story for an hour. And finally, Tara wished him good night and went to sleep.

"Good night, Tara," Kabir responded.

CHAPTER 24

Kabir's writing journey would be a cakewalk for him as he had decided to write an autobiographical novel. He prepared to put pen to paper as he rewound his thoughts to his childhood days and captured wonderful memories that he'd cherish. Upon writing, he thought of his mother and called her. "Hey! Hi, Mom."

She greeted, "Hello, Son. How are you?"

"I'm good here, Mom. But you know what? I've got a story."

"Wow! That's good news. But I have another good news for you."

Kabir queried, "What, Mom?"

She took a deep breath and said cheerfully, "Your partner is out of coma!"

Kabir couldn't believe his ears, so he squeaked, "What!"

She said, "Yup, he is out of coma and he is coming with us."

Kabir was in seventh heaven and was waiting to tell his partner all his stories. He gulped, "It's really great, Mom. So, when?"

She said, "Hmm…. Actually, we were planning to give you a surprise, but I'm your mom. I'm helpless. So, we are on the way to Nagpur. It will just take an hour before we reach home. Be ready to meet your partner, Son."

Kabir became nostalgic and had little time before his partner's homecoming. "Mom, I need to work. Okay, bye." He immediately put the receiver down and walked upstairs.

"Hey, Tara. Great news! Partner is coming back."

Tara, who was rehearsing for her dance festival, was excited to hear the news. "That's really a great news, Kabir."

Kabir moistened his lips and squeaked, "Ya, but the bad news is that they'll be here within an hour, miss. So, we need to make arrangement soon and get some stuffs around. Let's go."

Both the teens rode their bicycles and bought some cool stuffs to surprise Iyer.

The clock struck one; it was a scorching summer afternoon.

After an hour, a black sedan motioned in front of Mrs Kanta's house. All three got down from the car and walked through the pathway and reached the main entrance; Uncle Iyer pressed the doorbell, but no one came. After waiting for a minute, they realised that the door was open. They pushed the door and went inside, only to be surrounded by pitch darkness. It was really weird for them. And in a flash, the lights were switched on and glittering gold flakes tossed in air with a cheerful voice booming "Welcome home, partner."

Uncle Iyer was surprised to see Kabir. Kabir said with a contented voice "Hey, partner," and gave him a warm and tight hug. Both were crying seeing each other. Uncle Iyer grumbled, "Now, I have come na. Don't cry."

"Can you forgive me, partner?" Kabir asked.

Iyer, wiping his tears, said, "You hadn't made any mistake, pal." He patted and hugged him once again.

"Are you not going to welcome us?" his father joked. Kabir hugged his dad and mom with a smile from his teary face.

After controlling his emotions, Kabir wiped his eyes and gasped, "Let's go inside, partner."

Kabir dragged him to the hall where a cake and candles were placed. He handed the knife to him and said, "Partner, don't say no. Tara and I have prepared it together."

Okay, Tara, your friend, Iyer thought and gave a doubtful look.

"Partner, stop looking at me. Cut it na."

"Okay, fine." Iyer cut the cake and gave a piece to Kabir.

"Thank you, partner," said Kabir. All of them enjoyed the small homecoming party.

Kabir's mom found a good companion in the form of Mrs Kanta and soon the two started to converse. Dad and Iyer got themselves busy talking, resting in the sofa. And finally, Kabir and Tara were upstairs in Tara's room.

"So, now your parents have come. Now then?" Tara questioned, feeling upset.

"Then what? I will go to my house," Kabir squeaked.

Tara gasped and looked sad. Within a second, Kabir said, "Then what? I will go to my house and will come every day to your house. I guess I really need your help in completing my novel."

Tara was surprised and brightened her mood. Kabir clicked his tongue and said, "I mean I do really need your help for my novel. You are a part of my life—I mean of my novel."

Tara shied and smiled.

It was lunchtime, and Mrs Kanta forced Kabir's family to have their lunch in their home. With no choice left, everybody sat in the dining table and ate. For the first time, Kabir tasted Mrs Kanta's food and appreciated her, saying, "Aunt, it's really 'devastating.'"

All of them stared at Kabir, and he realised using the wrong word, so he said, "I...I...mean it's really awesome."

Everybody had a good laugh over the lunch. It was one of the best memories Kabir had with Tara.

CHAPTER 25

Finally, Kabir had a story to write with a new partner in tandem. Uncle Iyer decided to tease him on every chance he got.

"So, Tara is your new partner, hon?" Iyer teased, his eyes rolling.

"Hey, partner. She is just my friend."

"Okay, friend or something else," he taunted him.

"Stop teasing me, partner. Oops, it's six o'clock, I need to go." He took his diary and a pen.

Iyer noticed it and said, "Where? To Tara's?"

Suddenly, Kabir squeaked, "Shut up!" He was all smiles with a tinge of shyness.

Kabir went to Tara's room in upstairs. "May I come in, miss," Kabir teased.

Tara replied, "Of course, Mr Writer. Come in."

Kabir laughed and said, "I think I should call you Miss Singer."

Tara, with a grim smile, said, "Not so funny." Kabir managed to control his laughter to see her in a serious look.

He went and sat on the bed, and instantly, Tara ordered, "Not there, mister. Go and sit on the chair."

"Okay, okay." Kabir sat on the chair while Tara on the bed. They were face to face, with the irregular smiles.

"So, today we are going to start chapter one."

"Yes, miss," Kabir agreed, tapping his notebook.

"So, Mr Writer, start writing your life's journey from the beginning," Tara said.

"I was there inside my mother's belly for nine months before I came out. It was 17 November 20…"

"Fattu! You are not going to write a biography."

He giggled and said, "Okay, miss."

He enjoyed watching the new Tara, in a strict teacher behaviour. Since it wasn't dream, he couldn't take her for granted. They did their job quite well. Every day, Kabir spent one hour with Tara—sometimes in her house, sometimes in his house, and sometimes in the park on the wooden bench. Kabir's novel slowly and steadily took shape and size. With every chapter, Kabir's dream of becoming a writer materialised, and Tara's too.

***

It was Friday, and Kabir stayed late with Tara to finish his remaining chapters of the novel. They spent more than four hours and had dinner at her house. After the dinner, Kabir and Tara went to her room to complete the last chapter of his novel.

"Tara, I know up to this. What should I write next? I don't know what happened to me or with you."

Tara smiled and gasped, "Hmm… So, Mr Writer, don't know what to write?"

"I guess, I must go for a sequel. What do you say?"

"Don't be foolish. Those who don't know how to end a story write a sequel. But you know, so as I. Kabir, what do you think of us, just write it."

Kabir narrowed his eyes as he was confused. Tara grumbled, "I…I mean just write that 'their friendship turned into affection and they loved each other forever.'"

Kabir smiled and said, "Ya, I was also thinking of that." Tara took the pillow and hit him, knowing his intentions.

"Kabir, you will never change."

"Okay, okay. Sorry. Stop."

CHAPTER 26

"Tara, we did it. We did it, Tara!" Kabir excitedly told heron successful completion of his novel. After a month of hard work, he finally did it. Tara was quite happy to see Kabir in joyful mood. They held their hands together and danced and cheered along.

"Wait, wait. That's not the end. I need to publish it. I talked to my partner. He knows a man in Mumbai who is a publisher. I hope he will let my novel to be published," Kabir claimed.

"Hey, don't worry. No one is going to deny your work, Kabir," Tara praised with a smile.

"But promise me, you will give your first copy of book to me."

Kabir knelt and said, "I promise you, Tara." Kabir looked at her. Their eyes met, as time stopped in their world, and his lust, which visible in his eyes, was driven by love and affection for his only soulmate. His heart was racing, and he then stood up and gave a tight and intimate hug. She went into his arms, and stayed there for a long time, sharing their emotions and feelings for each other.

"I will miss you, Kabir."

Kabir held her face in his palms, kissed her forehead, hugged her once again and said, "Me too."

*

It was time to depart, and Kabir was confident of publishing his novel. Kabir put his luggage in the car's bonnet and was ready to go. Tara looked from her bedroom window. Kabir glanced at her and waved goodbye with a smile. *Hope you will come soon,* Tara thought, and wished him with a deep pain in her heart. He entered the car and said, "Partner, let's go."

This time, Uncle Iyer was confident about their travelling directions. But somehow old habits never change. Again, they were lost in the middle. Everywhere, there was jungle with greeneries and wild trees, and they wandered on the road. For the second time, they were stranded. They took help of Google Maps apps to finally reach Mumbai. "From next time onwards, we must go by train," Kabir insisted as the journey was quite long, and he was too tired to even get down from the car. However, Iyer took him to a restaurant and they had a great, refreshing supper. Both were so tired and spent the whole night in a hotel, except for Kabir, who went out roadside, taking his phone.

Hello, miss, Kabir texted. He clicked his tongue and waited for a minute.

Soon he got a text message as his phone buzzed: *Hey, Writer!*

So, how're you, miss?

Alive, I guess.

Kabir added thumps-up emoji with a text: *Well, me too.*

Are you missing me, miss?

Nope, I'm quite fine and good without the one whom I like.

I'm feeling nervous, Tara. I mean, what they would say about our work?

It's not ours, it's your hard work and passion. It's your dream, Kabir. You can't be nervous. Be confident and face it. Okay?

Yup. They texted each other for half an hour and soon Kabir felt sleepy. He texted, *okay then, miss. I guess I'm feeling sleepy after talking to you. So, good night.*

Hmm.

It's really disgusting when girls send "hmm," he thought and sent an angry-face emoji.

????

He again sent an angry-face emoji, and it was time for an emoji text-fight. They were now on their keypads with back and forth volley of emojis, which ended with Tara's victory.

Okay, good night. But how can I lose?

And finally, she texted: *It's all in your genes. Good night, fattu.*

Kabir giggled and went back to his hotel room for a peaceful sleep.

The next day was very special for Kabir. He woke up early and proofread his novel for any spell errors or typos. He soon got freshened up and was ready to meet the publisher. "Partner, I'm nervous."

"Partner, it's okay."

Iyer and Kabir went to the publishing house, and Kabir's heart pounded. He was nervous yet was confident. *What if they reject it? What if I come back home without publishing? What Tara would think?* These questions occupied his mind, and he started to shiver.

Uncle Iyer shook him and said, "Kabir, don't worry. Let's go."

They saw a huge building in front of them, almost touching the bluish sky. Kabir was surprised to see a skyscraper. Iyer patted his shoulder and signalled him to move inside. They entered the building and took a lift to the third floor. Kabir tried to calm down himself and did some push-ups. "Hey, partner, be confident. Okay?" Iyer said.

Whatever Iyer said, it went above Kabir's head. He closed his eyes and thought of Tara's face. *I'm with you, just go, Kabir,* he listened to his inner voice. He then opened his eyes with a smile on his face.

"Hey, Kabir, go," Iyer said to him, showing the door.

Kabir looked at Iyer and said, "Iyer, what do you think? Can I make it."

Uncle Iyer held his hands and said in a pleasing tone, "If you have hands, you can make anything. So just go." Iyer kissed him on his forehead and wished him luck as he pushed the door open.

Kabir cleared his throat before he entered the meeting room. The room was air-conditioned; he could feel the cool air caressing his face. He saw three gentlemen looking at him. He bit his lips, wished them and shook hands.

He took a seat and kept his manuscript on the table. The first person asked, "So, Kabir, right?"

Kabir nodded.

"Well, we read your novel and it's…" Kabir's heart was in his mouth.

"Well, it's not good. The plot is nice, story is nice, but it's too childish. What do you say?" He passed the copy of his novel to the second person, most probably the editor.

"Ya, your way of writing is quite different from all. This is 2017, and public can't be so ridiculous to read such immature books."

The third person in the room too claimed the same with a suggestion, "We think you should try reading more and improve and expand your vocabulary."

Kabir had never expected such answers from the publishers. He felt dejected and miserable, even pathetic. He felt lonely when his two inner characters came into being. Kabiroh claimed, *Kabir, what are you waiting for? Just slam them with your novels and leave the room.*

Kabirah insisted, *Kabir, be quiet. You know how to lure people. Just go on facts and give your novel a best look.*

Kabir clenched his fist and slammed the papers down on the table. The vibrations made the publishers to tremble. They were shocked to see his behaviour. His eyes reddened, and he posed an angry look on his face. He was rigid. He shouted at the panel members, "What do you know about my novel?" He once again slammed his novel down on the table. He made fist out of his hands and crushed the papers in front of him. His eyes were fixed on those three-black sheep. He sat on the table, close to them, and figured out. He moved towards the left and looked at the first person, "Ha-hah…What did you say? It is childish. You can't imagine. The day I was determined to complete this novel was the day I became matured."

He licked his lips and turned over and peered over the middle fellow. "And you, bloody shirt and tie. Public don't want, uh? A writer well knows about the reader's needs."

He stared the final member of the panel and mocked, "And you, Mr Vocabulary. Don't you know what's the meaning of vocabulary?"

Kabir laughed with a terrible scowl and got down from the table. He was upset with his own behaviour. He looked at his foot, then raised his head, and said in a sad tone, "I'm from Nagpur. But I came here only to publish. My dream was to write a novel only to meet Meera Sharma, but soon my dream became my desire and I lost my partner. I cried for him. After that I made a good friend in that course of time, but I have left her to meet you people and publish my novel."

Kabir wiped his tears and begged, "Sir, I want you to publish my novel. It's my request, sir. Please."

It was a heart-breaking scene; one of the panel members ran towards Kabir and held his face and looked at him. He waved over his teary-eyed face and said, "We have already read your story, it is fabulous. We were just kidding. I have never seen such a determined writer. We will surely publish your novel. Don't cry."

Kabir's face lit up with a smile, and he thanked the publishing team. Kabir once again thanked all the three persons and shook hands with them. While he left the room, he smiled at them and said,

"Thank you so much." The publishers gave a positive look and waved him goodbye. Kabir came out and saw Iyer. He ran towards him and hugged him forcefully. "You know what, partner? They are ready to publish my novel. I'm so much excited."

Iyer was happy to see him happy. "Told you," Iyer joked. They giggled, and Iyer said, "Okay, Kabir. I just need to talk to them about some more documents. Okay."

Kabir nodded and thought of Tara.

Tara, I do. He stopped and smiled at his thought.

***

They were back in the hotel when Iyer told him, "Partner, they said they would print200 copies at first and then seeing the rising demand they would print more copies."

"Shit, partner. It means they have to use more ink later," he giggled with his stupid comments.

Iyer laughed and said, "Sure, partner." The sun dipped below the horizon, and they closed their eyes, except Kabir (again).

He went out. It was cool and humid outside. The grass in lawn had early dew set in, and he felt it was a right place to sit and talk.

I told you, they can't deny your work.

Ya, but it was because of my brilliant acting.

C'mon, writer. By the way, Kabir—Kabir heard some disturbing sound from Tara's end; perhaps, she was in pain with aches.

Hey, Tara. Are you okay?

Kabir, there is something I must tell you... The phone fell down from Kabir's hand and broke into pieces. "Hey you, man! Can't you see?"

"Sorry, dear." He saw an old man with a stick.

"No, it's fine." Kabir collected the broken pieces of his mobile phone.

The next day, Kabir went to the publishing house and gave his idea for designing the book's cover page.

He requested the publisher if they could print one copy. Soon the manager came out and gave him the printed copy of his novel. It was wrapped in brown-coloured paper. Kabir slowly tore the wrappings and held it. It was his hard work, his desire, his six months of sweat and pain. He kept the book close to his chest and closed his eyes. *Now, that's the best feeling in the world,* Kabir thought.

CHAPTER 27

The publisher informed Kabir that they need a month's time to print more copies. It was already a month he hadn't returned to Nagpur. So Kabir decided to go back to redeem Tara's promise. On the way back, Kabir's thoughts occupied his mind. The one thought that was lurking his mind was about Tara's words: *Promise me, you will give your first book to me*. He thought, *Wow! It feels so good*.

Slowly and steadily, Iyer drove all the way, from Mumbai to Nagpur. After a long, arduous journey, Kabir was just15 minutes away from fulfilling Tara's promise. But the sky was overcast with thick cloud cover. There was a possibility of skies opening up any moment. Both strong winds and loud clap of thunders accompanied the darkened clouds, creating an eerie atmosphere, which made Kabir scared. But his mind being filled with thoughts of Tara made him smile. He and his partner somehow reached home. With no time to wait, he held the book and rushed to Tara's house. He knocked the door and cried, "Tara, it's me

Kabir." He was quite excited. He again knocked it, but there was no reply. He became worried and looked around and noticed that the door was locked. He looked around, being quite annoyed. He then went to her next-door neighbour.

"Aunty, where is Mrs Kanta?"

Aunt replied, "I don't know, Son."

Kabir was in a sullen mood, as his worries were bothering him. He knocked each and every house in that locality, walking door to door, but everyone's answer was in the negative.

One of the neighbourhood aunty told him, "Oh, Mrs Kanta? They all went somewhere."

"Aunt, do you have any idea where they have gone? Aunt, please. It's urgent," he beseeched.

"Sorry, dear, I don't know."

The word *I don't know* stabbed him badly.

Kabir lost his hope of seeing Tara. After so much of knocking and shouting, Kabir was knocked down by his life's terrible tragedy. He fell on his knees on the middle of the lonely road. He was shattered emotionally. The tears pricked his eye, slowly rolled over his cheek and fell on the book he kept in his hand. Soon tears welled up and drenched his book. He looked skyward and yelled, "TARA!" The cumulonimbus cloud broke the silence and poured heavily in sync with Kabir's tears. He was in terrible agony. He was now literally rain-soaked, which made him even more weaker. Iyer came and held his shoulder and made him stand. Before Iyer could say anything, Kabir's teary-eyed face combined with dirt and mud shivered, and he once again cried out, "Iyer, she cheated me."

Looking at his pathetic condition, Iyer thought he was a victim of foul play. He held his cheeks and said, "Kabir, don't worry. She will come back."

"No, partner, she…" Kabir couldn't express his pain, so he hugged his partner tightly. The rain was unstoppable the entire night and flooded the entire area.

*

Kabir lay on his bed feeling tired. Uncle Iyer came and held his hands and whispered, "Kabir." He half-opened his eyes. He looked pale and weak. Iyer muttered, "Partner, are you all right?"

Kabir made himself comfortable by arranging his pillow to his shoulders and straightening his body. Soon tears trickled down his cheeks. He then uttered, drowning in his sorrow, "Partner, she is gone."

Due to continuous crying, his voice had become weak and inaudible, Iyer felt. He waved his hair and said, "She will come soon, partner."

Kabir said, "I promised her to show my first copy. I can't publish my book until I show it to Tara. I must find her at any cost." All of a sudden, he got out of his bed, walked bare-footed through the green fields, and reached the park and sat on the wooden bench. He was in deep thought and planned to find her.

He thought, *Okay, I need to find her.* After reflecting upon the happenings of the previous day, he fully comprehended the situation and decided to make a full-fledged search. He once more went back to her house and inspected for every odd and ends, like a note or a letter, but it was waste of time.

It was one week since Tara's vanishing act, still Kabir has not come to his senses. He then consulted Gauri regarding Tara's whereabouts.

"Sorry, Kabir, she didn't tell me anything about it."

"No, it's okay." (It wasn't actually.)

Publishers were breathing down his neck to finalise the publishing date, promotional tours, and so on and so forth. This was purgatory of sorts for Kabir as he experienced a life of hell. Every day, he tried to get some information about her whereabouts, but soon he ran out of luck. His broken phone was repaired. After three weeks of love conquest, he left it. Yes, he did leave it.

If she really ever cared about me, then she must have called me once.

***

Iyer mumbled, "Partner, your book will be published all over the country. And she will definitely read it and will surely feel proud of you."

Kabir was silent and felt emotionally crippled. He turned away and ignored Iyer's talk.

Iyer was helpless too, so he left the room. *How can she leave? Was there any problem? She would have told me either? Where are you, Tara?* Kabir thought and dozed off.

The rain had stopped as night drew, and another torrid day had ended. Kabir blinked and woke up. He scratched his head and glanced at the clock; it was eleven. He'd had shrunken face and dry eyes. He took a deep breath, holding his pillow close to his chest.

After a second, he walked downstairs and knocked the door of Iyer's room. Uncle Iyer was in deep sleep, as usual. He opened the door on the second knock, feeling irritated. Licking his lips, he saw Kabir and then at the clock and got confused. "Well, partner. I will publish. I will show Tara that I'm not a coward. I will show her that I, Kabir Malhotra, have a lot of potential to fight and win. I will show her. Yes, I will."

Iyer felt happy for Kabir. He hugged him and promised him, "Your book will surely inspire many people."

CHAPTER 28

AFTER FOUR MONTHS

The youngest bestseller of India, Kabir Malhotra, was the headlines all over the country, in every dailies and news channels. In less than two months more than one lakh copies were sold. Kabir became a household name. His friends circle expanded. The public gathered in front of his house and took selfies with him. The media crew rounded his house 24/7. It became hard for Kabir to even step out of his house. His book, *I Want to Be a Writer*, inspired a million. The publishers were happy as they made huge profits. Kabir's parents were happy, Iyer teased him by calling him *sir*. Everybody was happy except Kabir.

He went on a book tour to every major city in India as per the publishing deal. People all over the country loved him. His novel got excellent reviews from the readers. He was the trending topic in social media, bombarded with messages and tweets. One news channel described his novel as: *Kabir truly gave his heart to his devastating story. Well written with tenderness and love. It will push the readers to make their dreams as their desires.*

He faced cameras and gave interviews, day in and day out. He was only free during night-time. In the silence of the midnight, every day, he hid himself in his room and cried under his pillow. Tara's memory killed him, lurking him like an incurable cancer. Nevertheless, he kept his chin up.

"Look, we want such children like Master Kabir Malhotra as our role model," the principal praised.

While going home, Krish and Bob saw him going alone with a lost face.

During a book launch event in Mumbai, Kabir became nervous seeing a crowd of youngsters. A well-shaved fair boy from the crowd asked, "Kabir sir, why did you think of writing a story?"

Kabir mused and said, "First of all, don't call me sir. I'm just16 only. I should call you brother." The crowd laughed on hearing his innocent reply.

Kabir looked down, inhaled and said, "Well, I wasn't a born writer. I had a dream of meeting Meera Sharma, but when it became a strong desire, I don't know."

The crowd clapped and raised their hands to ask him more questions. "Okay, you." Kabir pointed to a boy who stood in the middle of the crowd with his book. "Sir. Sir. Sorry sir. I mean,

Kabir. Who is Tara, the girl to whom you dedicated this book?"

Kabir was taken aback with this question, as his heart fluttered remembering Tara. He said nervously, "She...She was my friend." With that answer, he rushed out of the place and boarded the car and squeaked, "Iyer, I want to go. I can't live here. Let's go."

Iyer, with a worried look, asked, "But what happened, partner?"

Kabir yelled, "Just go!" Iyer steered the car and drove back home. Kabir was calm and sad. He just wanted to be alone. And God helped him as Iyer for the third-time lost track of the direction in the middle of a forest. None were there, and there was not even mobile network. They were alone.

Iyer was scared and began to shiver. His hands turned icy cold and breathed heavily. He looked beside and said, "Kab..." But Kabir was not there.

He looked at the back seat and searched for Kabir. He fingered the steering wheel and looked through his right window. "Hey, Kabir."

Iyer gazed at him. He sat on a stone surrounded by trees and creepers. The bushy grasses added greenery to the background. Iyer walked and sat beside him.

Kabir looked at the overcast sky. He asked, "Iyer, if God knows our problems, then why don't he solve it all?"

Iyer twitched his mouth and implied, "Well, I don't know whether he exists or not, but the faith on him helps us to deal with our problems. When I was in coma, I never felt like I'm living. But I was having faith not on God, but on me. This faith helped me to get cured. It means I didn't cure myself. It was the faith that one day I will wake up and could run that cured me."

Kabir's life was screwed up, rather messed up. He exhaled with a sigh and said, "It's so easy to tell na. But in practice, it gets too much complicated with the slippery threads of life."

"Maybe not."

Kabir was fed up with his boring life—without entertainment, without fun, without Tara.

Kabir and Iyer finally saw a woodcutter passing through the plateau and asked him the direction. Soon they were on the road, and Iyer drove with no further hiccups.

CHAPTER 29

It had been five months, Kabir hadn't seen Tara. No phone calls, no messages, nothing. His friends pestered him for new books and stories, but Kabir's thoughts were on Tara.

It was a bright and sunny day. Kabir was walking along a tree-lined street when a matte black car passing through the street stopped on seeing him. Soon the car's window screen pulled down to reveal the face of one and only Meera Sharma! Kabir stood still and was absolutely shocked to see his idol. Kabir couldn't believe on his faith and destiny. Meera smiled at him, but Kabir's voice trembled as he began to speak.

"Hello, Kabir," Meera started her conversation.

"Oh! Is it true?" Kabir pinched himself to confirm that it wasn't a dream. He still stared at her; meanwhile, Meera got down from her car and walked towards him.

"Hey, Kabir?" For a second, Kabir remembered Tara's sweet voice.

He looked upward and swallowed. "Hello, mam, I'm your biggest fan and—"

Meera interrupted and said, "Let's sit and talk." Kabir nodded.

They went to his house in Meera's car, and Iyer was glad to see her. Dad and Mom were excited, couldn't believe their eyes.

She sat on the sofa, and Mom offered her coffee. Kabir was a bit nervous but acted as if he was normal.

Before Meera could start a conversation, Kabir made a plan, so he greeted, saying, "I'm so much happy to see you here, mam. Let me take you to my room. You will be stunned to see my collection."

Meera nodded with a smile. They went upstairs, and Kabir hurried inside his room and sprayed room freshener to get rid of putrid odour.

Meera entered the room and was surprised to see his collection of books. He had complete set of Meera's books in his bookshelf, along with books of other famous Indian and foreign authors. She was really impressed. "So, Mr Writer, what's next?"

Kabir blinked, not knowing what to answer. *What she is asking?* Kabir thought.

Meera licked her lips and asked, "I mean, what are the plans for your next book. I may help you out."

Kabir gave a pleasing look and confessed, "No, mam. That's all, I can't write anymore."

Meera wasn't happy with his answer. She claimed, "Why Kabir?"

Kabir didn't want to respond to her question, which obviously showed on his face. Meera deciphered something was wrong with Kabir, so she went near and cupped his face with her hand and asked in a motherly manner, "Look at me. Tell me what happened?"

Kabir's was on the cusp of crying, and he stayed mum. Meera waited for his answer, but Kabir was in no mood to open his mouth. With a dull face, she said, "Okay, then. Good luck with your book. See you."

Meera was halfway down the room, when he finally said, "She was Tara…"

Meera turned and listened to his statement. Kabir then narrated his whole story, every bit of it. After an hour-long telling of his heart-breaking story, he collapsed in her arms, shedding tears. Meera was clueless and took a deep breath and looked up. She saw his tear-soaked face and said, "Kabir."

Kabir wiped his tears and nodded.

"Did you try to find her?"

Kabir shied to answer her and remained silent. Then after a minute, he said, "Mam, she cheated me, she is—"

Meera smiled and said, "Okay! Then who are you, mister? You thought that if she is gone, then she cheated you. Then you are wrong, Mr Writer."

"You know what? People always do a great mistake when they start judging others. Who knows about their situation. We think *what we see* and *what we hear* are always true and right, but it isn't."

Outside, in the street, they heard a car screeching to halt, almost ramming ata drunkard. Kabir and Meera watched from by the upstairs window. The car driver foul-mouthed the helpless guy and warned him, "Bloody lazybones, go and die anywhere else."

The crowd gathered as mere spectators and enjoyed the happenings. After five minutes of back and forth of mouthing expletives, the driver drove his car and the drunken man zigzagged his way unconsciously.

Again, Meera and Kabir were inside the room and sat face-to-face. Meera asked, "So, Kabir, what do you think of that drunken man?"

Kabir claimed, "He must be a very careless, cheap fellow."

Meera smirked and rolled her eyes and started, "Kabir, that's your problem. You see the scene or the event but do not understand the situation. Okay, tell me, what do you know about the drunkard. He might have lost his wife or children.

There's a lot of backstory—pain and sorrow—we don't know, but everybody has some sort of opinion. But the thing we can do to help those is by staying positive. That's all."

Kabir was confused. Meera held his hands and said, "Okay, let me show you."

They left the house, and Meera searched for that drunkard. She saw him near the signal crossing towards the highway. Meera looked at the red light and ran to reach him, in which she succeeded. She then grabbed his shirt from the neck and dragged him.

He screamed, "What are you doing? I don't want to live anymore. For whom should I live?" he cried his heart out.

Meera worried for him and asked, "But what happened?" And Kabir looked confused.

The man cleared his throat and said, "Nothing to say, only to regret."

Meera straightened his shoulders and made him to lean towards the roadside wall and sit and enquired him once again.

"Okay," he said, "I had a son. A great child with a gifted mind and a kind and gentle soul. He never wanted anything, except knowledge. He topped the class, and I wished him to become a doctor. He did work hard and cracked the entrance test with flying colours. We all were happy and content. But he got into bad association in his college and got addicted to drugs. We gave him drug therapy counselling to get him back to his old ways, but his health has taken a huge toll. Today, the medical counsellor called me and said Harsh had committed suicide."

He cried and told his painful story of his beloved son. Kabir and Meera felt sorry for him. Meera patted his shoulder and said, "Sir, you have your wife to live for. You can't give up. Go and give a hug to your wife, you will learn everything."

The man wiped his tears and took a brisk walk, without any reply.

After his departure, Meera looked at Kabir, as he was certainly disturbed. She questioned, "Now, tell me, why Tara left you?"

Kabir looked at his surrounding and found thousands of people. He was astonished to know each had their own stories—some happy and some sad.

Kabir scratched his head, looking confused. For a few seconds, he closed his eyes and thought, and then he claimed, "I got it. Oh! Holy shit. She repeatedly told me to come soon. Ah!"

Kabir added, "She…She wanted to be a dancer and…and…I promised her that I will help."

Kabir grabbed the phone and searched for some information. He said surprisingly, "If I'm not wrong, it's in a month's time."

"So, what are you going to do now?" Meera asked. Kabir looked straight at her, with hope and confidence. He said, "I'm going to Chandigarh."

CHAPTER 30

Kabir wanted to find out Tara at any cost. Meera, Iyer and Kabir talked about his travel and his plan of finding her.

"Partner, I have done a mistake, let me resolve it. I will go alone."

Iyer looked worried and grieved, "Great! Now you want to go alone? When you were small, I took you everywhere, every night for ice creams and cool drinks. And now you..." (Blackmailing Part 1)

Kabir was silent and looked at the floor. Knowing his dilemma, Meera stood up and said, "Okay, we all will go. I really want you to complete your real-life story. So, I will help you. In Chandigarh I have a friend, we can stay there for a day."

When people with helping tendency joined each other, nuisances arrived too in the form his freakish friends. Krish and Bob returned after a short holiday and knocked the door.

"Hey, Kabir, whose car is this?" Bob cried; on the other hand, Krish identified the women to whom the car belongs to and went to take a selfie.

"Hey, Kabir. Am I dreaming?"

Kabir nodded and gripped his fingers. "Mam, let's go to my home. It's nearby this way…"

She greeted, "Sorry, champ, I need to go. I mean—we need to go."

Krish and Bob narrowed their eyes on Kabir, and Kabir explained them everything (once again).

"We will also go," Krish muttered.

"You can't. You—"

Krish interrupted, "We are your childhood friends. Lately, you're very sad and in pain. Your life has changed. We feel bad for you. So, we will go. Okay." (Blackmailing Part 2)

"But…"

"Nothing more to say. I'm also going to complete your story. And I had heard that in Chandigarh there are a lot of pretty girls."

Kabir smiled and hugged them. "Tara, I'm coming," Kabir whispered to himself.

Meera parked her car near Kabir's house. Iyer loaded the luggage in the boot of the car, and all the five were ready for the journey. The car drove slowly through the street and accelerated down the national highway. This time around, Iyer was focussed and was very much clear of his direction as he had Google Maps handy. During the journey, everyone took turn to sleep: Kabir slept thrice and Meera twice. But poor Iyer, his concentration was all on the roads. After 20 hours of tiring journey, they reached the perfect city of the world, and India's city beautiful and cleanest city—Chandigarh.

They reached in time, thanks to Iyer's marathon driving, and stayed at Meera's friend's house. That night Kabir didn't get a wink of sleep. He felt the presence of Tara in Chandigarh. He went to terrace and felt the cool and gentle breeze caress his face.

"So, Mr Writer, can't sleep, eh?" Meera teased him.

Kabir giggled and said, "No."

Kabir fingered the boundary of the parapet and hissed, "What will she do after meeting me? It's been seven months, she might have forgotten me."

Meera came closer to him and said, "Hey, Kabir. Friendship is not measured by days but by depths."

Kabir giggled and coughed, "Mam, you and your quotes!"

Kabir's eyes brightened with tears and Meera saw it. She joked, "Haven't you proposed her?"

Kabir looked at her and laughed, "What!"

Meera composed herself and said, "Okay, okay, fine." And after a second, she again enquired, "Have you ever kissed her?"

Kabir cheeks turned red and hot with shyness. He howled, "Mam, you," and chased her down.

Dashing down the hall, Meera grunted, "Okay, okay, I'm sorry."

The night turned out to be eventful with good laughs and endless chatter.

CHAPTER 31

Friends never make a work easier, they make it the easiest. Krish and Bob searched the entire city with her photo. Iyer was instructed by Kabir to not to venture out and be at home, and Meera and Kabir went out with a mission to find her. They circled the whole city twice within a week without any clue. It frustrated everyone, as they were out of their comfort zone—out of their city, out of their family and out of their school.

"I can't make it," Kabir said, as he threw her photo at the tea stall and looked at his aching feet. Krish, Bob and Meera too were tired.

But Meera wanted Kabir to not lose hope and keep the momentum going, so she said, "Kabir, you can't give up. Okay."

But Kabir was hurt, mentally and physically. He ran from the stall in frustration as he couldn't able to find his other half; instead, the problem blew in proportion as days went by with no luck whatsoever. He at last sat on the bench on the nearby patio with his hopes broken.

Suddenly, he saw some middle-aged woman crossing his path. With no doubt, Kabir knew who she was: Mrs Kanta. Kabir was elated as well as shocked to see her and stood with stunned silence. Mrs Kanta too was motionless, twitching her lips.

After a minute or so of silence, Kabir rushed near to her and said, "Where is Tara?"

Hope and love spread from the corner of his eyes, and Mrs Kanta could feel his heart's saying and longing. She tried to explain him how all the events unfolded, but Kabir was in no mood to listen.

"Kabir, beta, she...she is..."

"Where is Tara?" Kabir demanded in harsher tone.

She swallowed hard and told at length at the entire story in one stretch.

"I was there, when her family met with the accident. She lost her father and her brother. And she was alone. That accident took a huge toll on her leg, causing a torn ligament, which she ignored. But now that the injury has aggravated, she is dying with pain. I do want her to be fine again. But she can't. Her dream is to participate in India's biggest dance festival, but the doctor has suggested that if she dances, it might cause heavy swelling that may lead to amputating her right leg."

Mrs Kanta sobbed. Kabir too felt the pain as his eyes grew wet. He enquired, "Where is she now?"

"A week before, while dancing she fell as gangrene set in her leg. I admitted her to the hospital that night. Now she is in the hospital. And I can't arrange cash for the operation...."and she collapsed on the grass.

"Hey, Aunt!" Kabir was unable to handle her heavy figure, but managed to take her to his house, and all the four—Meera, Iyer, Kanta and Kabir—talked about her health condition.

"She is fine," Meera suggested on seeing her medical reports.

Bob and Krish were glad to know Tara was in Chandigarh, and there stood Kabir in deep silence. Iyer left his coffee on the table, came near Kabir and said, "Let her be fine. And we are going to find her."

"Yup, sure."

Kabir went to his room and took out his phone. He fell back on the bed and browsed the photo gallery of him and Tara together. He smiled, *So, cute we were.* He then played a recording he had saved that day as "My first call."

So, Mr Writer. Are you scared? No, I'm not. You can. Believe. Kabir was moved to tears hearing her voice. Sometimes, we feel the past was cruel, but time makes us to realise the right thing at the right time (always).

After an hour, Kabir heard someone calling him loudly.

"Kabir, hurry up." He dashed down to the living room; and Aunt uttered, "Tara is in Caringbird Hospital."

And Kabir fled. He ran for his friendship, for his love and for his promise. He reached the hospital and enquired the receptionist about a patient named Tara.

"She is in Room No5."

Kabir sprinted and looked for Room No 5. He saw the door number with the number plate 5 and pushed the door slowly. The hinges of the door creaked open. Kabir gasped as he got a glimpse of Tara's face after so many months. Tara lay on the bed, motionless and still unconscious with ventilator and glucose drips stand around her bed. Her face was dry but still cute. Kabir touched her cold hands and sat nearby her in a chair. He then held her hands and kissed it. Kabir felt rejuvenated on seeing her pleasing face. There was nothing to regret though he had made a mistake. He left her hands with regret and soon rushed back to the hospital counter and enquired regarding operation fees.

"Only 10 lakhs, sir," the front-desk girl in the bills section.

Kabir, unable to control his emotion, thought of finding solution for paying the money. He then got a great idea. He immediately called Iyer and told him to transfer 10 lakhs—the money that he made from selling his novel—to the hospital account without any delay.

"Thank you, sir."

"Don't call me sir. Okay?"

She nodded and Kabir left the hospital premise. He still cried but consoled himself as he was reignited by the sweet memories of Tara, the time he spent with her. He rested on the garden bench where he had been that morning and was about to take a nap when a hand slipped from behind and patted his shoulder, voicing, "Hey, second partner."

Kabir looked at him and glanced, "You, Uncle! What a pleasant surprise! I mean how?" Kabir rubbed his eyes.

"Yup, I know, I have been here for some family work, and I guess I'm lucky that you met me."

Kabir wanted to smile, but he didn't.

"So, second partner, tell me. Now, what happened?"

Kabir was desolate yet contented, with chaotic events disturbing his life's hopes. He swallowed hard and said tearfully, "I'm broken." He then narrated his sad story.

On hearing his story, Uncle replied, "Listen, Kabir, it's not a problem, unless you highlight it. I know it's too tough to be like that again—that is, what you were with her months ago. But don't lose her. She might not love you, as she used to, but I know you can, as you did earlier."

He took a stick and gave it to him. "Break it," he said. Kabir broke it in a flash. Then the old man took bundle of sticks and gave it to Kabir to break.

"I know. It will not break. I have read the story many a times when I was small."

"Yup, that's good. But what did you learn from it?"

Kabir said, "That, together we stay, we are strong."

The old man glanced and gave him thorn-filled sticks and asked him to break.

It was impossible to break, he knew. Kabir failed in it. And the old man said, "It is true that we are strong when we are united. And I must say that the sticks are the memories which are going to make us strong."

"How?"

The old man giggled and said, "Simple. Our past teaches us lessons. And we become strong."

Kabir nodded.

"But the moment I get a stick full of thorns, it makes me stronger. That is one of the bad memories of the past which makes us the strongest. Tara might be your hardest past, yet the strongest which do not require any other stick to be harder."

"And, my friend, always remember that cruel past reaps a positive present, like a rose with thorns."

Kabir was confused but nodded his head.

"What are you waiting for? Make your novel a reality. End up like you did in your novel. Go and make her that crazy girl, what she was. Go and sober her, like she did. And above all, go and promise her to be with her. Always."

"Now go, second partner!"

Kabir ran miles and reached Caringbird Hospital, because he needed no reason to be with Tara. He entered the room and held her hands. He smiled and pressed her hands upon his chest and cried.

"Sorry, Tara."

Kabir could see slight moment in her eyes, and in a while slowly she gathered her consciousness and lifted open her eyes. She had blurry vision. She did see Kabir at once and gave a weak smile. Kabir could see in her eyes her desire to live this life.

She tried to speak but struggled. Kabir, who was completely exhausted, went near to hear her mumbling.

"Now, you are a good actor, Mr Writer."

Kabir's eyes pooled with happy tears as he heard her voice in aeons. He pressed her hands hard and gasped, "Tara, why you did that?"

Tara uttered something. Kabir bent his neck to listen.

"It's all in my genes." Kabir cheered, and let his lips caress her forehead.

"I'm really sorry, Tara."

Tara smiled and said, "Hey, Kabir. It was my fault."

"No, it was mine."

"Okay then, go to hell. I don't want to talk to you."

Kabir was happy to see Tara. He learned that there is nothing to hide or to reveal, because the day we were born was the day we all were revealed. Life is too great to live for some reasons. But Kabir didn't make any reason for his living, as there was Tara at every moment of his life. Sometimes, we will feel the loneliness consuming us, but the day we start believing that the reason is grand, we start living the life to the fullest.

Kabir heard a lot of things from Tara.

***

Tara was back to her normal self with her crazy attitude and funny character. She might not get a chance to perform in the dance festival, but she'd found a true and genuine friend—a friend who can go any distance for her wellness, a friend who can handle any critical situation and bring smiles to her face, a friend who can fight the whole world and stand in support of her all the time.

EPILOGUE

⚶ ⚶ ⚶

"I can still remember that day and that triumph flourishing upon my face. It's...It's not just a memory, it's much worthier than it."

He licked his lips and a sweet tear ran down his cheeks. He sniffed and looked at her. He patted his thighs with anxiety and confessed, "So, it's over?"

She wiped her wet eyes and said, "Your story is beyond your book." Kabir smiled and took the last sip of his coffee.

He sat back and chuckled, "Mainly, I liked that part when Gauri gave a hug to me, and it was awful to see Tara's face."

The interviewer glanced, but she grimaced. She swallowed hard and pointed him towards his back, but Kabir, without listening to her sign, again claimed, "Leave that, you know, it was more awesome to see her face when she asked me whether I wanted to learn painting from her or not. Stupid!"

He rolled over laughing, while the interviewer pointed him to look towards his back. His laughter subdued, and in the back stood TARA, staring at him!

He again swallowed hard and uttered, "Actually, Tara, she thought me I was a truthful and an honest boy. So, to prove her wrong, I...I was just lying to her."

Tara stood with her hands on her curves and yelled furiously, "I came here to call you. It's been six and we had already decided to go."

Kabir remembered the promise he'd made and took a leave. "Mam, I promised her, I can't break the promise. I need to go."

Kabir stretched his T-shirt and lowered the jeans. While he was leaving, the interviewer stood and asked, "But where?"

Kabir turned and responded, "Just to face my fear. I mean for a ROLLER-COASTER RIDE!"

Tara and Kabir walked a few metres when Tara noticed a book in his right hand.

"Kabir, what is that?"

Kabir looked at the book and said, "Oh, this one. It's for my second partner."

Tara looked confused, and Kabir knew it. He muttered, "Actually, when I was all alone, when both you and Iyer were absent from my life, I met an old man. He told me his story but was proud of it. He was calm and gave a new lease of life to me."

Kabir licked his lips and continued, "You know what? If he was not there at that time, then writing must have become hard for me. But he really helped me in the time of need. So, I'm going to gift all my books to him."

Tara was impressed with Kabir's reply.

They reached his home, and an old woman opened the door, looking tired. Kabir looked at her and whispered, "Where is Uncle?"

With no reply, the elderly woman welcomed them inside and asked them to have a seat. They went around the house. The old woman served them a glass of water, and Kabir implied, "Okay, Aunt, where is Uncle? I need to give him these books. He really helped me a lot."

The old woman looked confused and confessed in a low voice, "Beta, what are you talking about?"

Before Kabir could respond to her, Tara patted on his shoulder and pointed towards the wall. Kabir then stood up and went near. He saw a picture of the Uncle that read: *Amrit Varma, India's greatest philosopher and writer, died in 2000.*

"WHAT!"

ABOUT THE AUTHOR

A simple boy of 17, with a creative mind and extraordinary thoughts, trying to create a realistic world of friendship and love. I want to be a writer is his debut novel inspired by true events around him.